La Petite Negress

An Historical Fictional Tale in Verse

By

SHELAAGH

Cover Illustration: Neil Ross
www.limbolo.net

Botanical Scribe™2013©2017 by Three Islands Press
www.3ip.com

Portrait photograph: Amy Barnard
www.amybarnardphotography.com

Publicity: Cameron Publicity and Marketing
www.cameronpm.co.uk

Published by
Silent Fizz Media

www.silentfizzmedia.com

ISBN: 978-1-9997587-0-7

Dedicated to my late mother Mrs Hilda Maud Ferrell affectionately known as Miss Mabel Harris to her family. She blessed my childhood ears with poetry. I remain eternally grateful.

ACKNOWLEDGEMENTS

I would like to acknowledge all the unwavering support and encouragement I have received for this book from its creative beginnings to its completion. When I started writing in the UK, my day job required me to travel regularly on long train journeys around the country with various colleagues. To while away the hours I would read a chapter or so, of the work in progress on the train. My colleagues would listen. When I was about to stop for fear I was encroaching on their time they would urge me to continue. As the story came to an abrupt halt, their reaction was a combination of intrigue and frustration as they wanted to know what happened next. They begged me to finish the book. Over time extracts of the manuscript were read to friends and family in the UK and my adopted home in the USA. The reaction seemed identical irrespective of nationality, class, gender or race. Yet at times I would lose confidence in my ability and it seemed outsiders had more belief in my skill than I had in my own. There was a writing hiatus after I moved to the USA. However, again I was encouraged to complete the book before returning to the UK.

I would like to give a Very Special Thankyou to: The Reverend Joy Price and St Paul's United Methodist Church, Tarzana, Los Angeles. Revd Joy Price offered me a room to write that enabled me to complete the book; To her husband Gordon Sheldall for his generous support; To my dear friend Jim Benham who has taken the time to read and comment on every draft of the story; To my dear friend Mary-Ann Cockburn for her exhaustive notes and corrections; To Neil Ross for his inspirational cover artwork; To my publicist Ben Cameron.

Thanks to: my father, Dennis Ferrell, my sister, Anthea Ferrell, Sam Snape, Helen Dowson Benjoya, gemmologist Roderick Mackenzie, Gloria Myles, Yvonne Deutschman-Hunt, Merrick Hunt, Simon Callow, David Wood, Nik Powell, Martin Kiszko, Ann McMulkin, Warren Wills, Dr Katrina Wood, Avril Scott Johnson,

Dorothy Scott, Michelle Scott, Barbara Hamilton, Tania Anderson, Gifty Annette Dubois, Diana and Bruce Gelvin, Mark Walker, Michael Addison, Heidi Langmead, Ereni Mendrinos, Alden McCalla, Sylbourne Sydial, Jane Reid, Andre Austin, Yasmeen Tabusum, the late Mrs Marguerite Johansen Deane, Mollie Tanner, Revd Steve Petty, Revd Joseph Choi and members of the Northridge United Methodist Church, Revd Audrey Browne, Revd Paul Hill and members of the Gospel Oak Methodist Church, Millfield School, Goldsmiths College, University of London, The Arts Educational Schools, Tanwood School and Picton House School for Girls. Finally Thank you to all my dear family, friends, teachers and work colleagues (you know who you are) in the UK, USA and around the world, unmentioned here but acknowledged in my heart for providing so much support and encouragement in the past and present for this book.

I am of mixed Caribbean cultural heritage, my mother Jamaican by birth and my father Guyanese. I grew up in the South West of England at a time when Black History had not yet been adopted as part of the curriculum in UK schools. Filling the gap in London was the New Beacon bookshop, a small independent bookshop located in Finsbury Park. The specialist shop and its publishing house New Beacon Books was founded in the 1960"s. by the late John La Rose and his wife Sarah White. When I moved to North London in the mid-eighties it was the "go to" place for anyone interested in African Caribbean literature. It was there that I purchased a book compiled by Nigel File and Chris Power entitled, *Black Settlers in Britain 1555-1958* that sparked my interest in Eighteenth century Black Britain. The book referenced the James Somerset Case 1772 and highlighted with a newspaper clipping, a subsequent event that took place following the court victory of the named slave. "According to the Public Advertiser 27 June 1772:

> *On Monday near 200 Blacks, with their Ladies, had an Entertainment at a Public Houſe in Weſtminster to celebrate the Triumph which their Brother Somerſet had obtained over Stuart his Maſter. Lord Mansfield's Health was echoed round the Room and the Evening concluded with a Ball. The Tickets for Admittance to this black Aſſembly were 5s. each.*

It played on my mind for years as I wondered, 'Who organized this event?' 'Who were those people that attended?' 'How did they earn enough money to pay for this Ball?' I could not answer those questions. However, fuelled with fascination my imagination eventually got to work.

La Petite Negress is an original historical fictional story set in the late 18th Century for the most part in London where the black community numbered around 20,000. Though not expressly about the James Somerset Case, the year 1772 presents a fine backdrop for the narrative in which the Somerset Case is elegantly woven. The narrative follows the adventures of La Petite's survival in England in 1772 with her twin brother following their escape from slavery in colonial Jamaica. La Petite and her brother land free but are undocumented strangers in unfamiliar territory. Where does that lead? I asked myself as the story seemingly began to write itself.

La Petite Negress is a novel written in verse. When it came to the actual writing style of the piece I believe composer John Adams had more influence on my stylistic choices than any literary wordsmith. I began my career as a performer in Musical Theatre in England. At one point I performed the role of Leila at the Royal Opera House, Covent Garden in the London Premiere Production of John Adams chamber musical *I Was Looking at the Ceiling and Then I Saw the Sky* with a libretto by June Jordon. Before starting work on this score, I believed I was fairly competent at counting bars of music. However, with a John Adams score it is not so straight forward as Adams continually and unexpectedly changes time-signatures within the framework of a set piece. It is not uncommon to see four different time-signatures in one phrase alone. Because of this, I felt I had no clear frame of reference upon which to memorise the music. Furthermore, unlike most typical music theatre scores, no line in the instrumental score mirrored the lines of the vocals being sung. While I rehearsed with the extremely gifted British composer and conductor, John Jansson I struggled to comprehend how what I was singing actually fitted into the orchestral arrangement and was losing faith until the day before the show's opening when I listened to a playback of my performance with the full orchestra for the first time. What I heard blew me away. The score that had seemed so complicated to learn did not sound complicated when listened to. It sounded immensely beautiful and moving. I was stunned. More importantly I felt an overall rhythmical fluidity that I had never experienced in music before. I never imagined Adams's choices would fundamentally create this amazing effect.

It was soon after my completed run, the inspiration came for *La Petite Negress* to be written in verse. For some random reason my understanding of John Adams's *Ceiling/Sky* score gave me reassurance that it would be possible to create a written work in verse that could have a fluid, naturalistic feel and sound when read. My experience gave me the courage to not be a slave to metre and measure and allow the narrative itself to determine the rhyming patterns and rhythmical flow. Once this was established in my mind, I could express my story in verse with relative ease. Today I feel I must give credit to my John Adams musical experience and thanks to those who cast me and worked with me on the production. I honestly believe that if I had not been exposed to the work, I would never have come up with the idea to write *La Petite Negress* and would never have had the confidence to follow through with the eccentric nature of the verse. Unsurprisingly, I felt during the writing process, I was principally writing an audiobook.

With regards the title, I am often asked if there should be a letter "e" at the end of "Negress". I studied a little French and still I do not believe so. The creative title "La Petite Negress" should be viewed as an English title not a French one and as such can be interpreted and understood more accurately for what it is in English than would be the case if correctly written in French. In French, "La Petite Negresse" would become a small child and La Petite is not a small child and this is not ostensibly a "children's" book.

La Petite Negress is a pacey, lyrical adventure. I hope the book informs, inspires but most of all entertains. Enjoy!

TABLE OF CONTENTS

PROLOGUE

18th Century Europe: colonial powers are slave trading
Abolitionists in Britain are vehemently campaigning
To bring about closure to this cruel, ghastly business
And the global madness caused by greed fuelled sickness

The economic spoils are currently being made
Through a system best known as the "triangular trade"
Ports across three continents create the triangle
Europe, Africa and the Americas at each angle

The shipping lanes used that determine the flow
Were mapped out by the Portuguese centuries ago
Their pioneers did dominate "the age of sail"
They were able to determine how the winds prevail

And noted down, for reference, the currents of the seas
While voyaging to and from the Colonies
Bearing this in mind and that having been said
Here is how Britain operates the first, second and third leg:

Ships leave English ports head south to West Africa
With a cargo load of trinkets, beads, cloth, ammo, guns and copper
The goods are sold or bartered and the profits made pay
For the purchase and transporting of African slaves

The ships now sail "The Middle Passage" going east to west
Below the 30th parallel north route thought to be the best
(Due to the favourable "trade winds" of the Westerlies
That propelled the slave ships faster to the West Indies)

SHELAAGH

Slaves are then off loaded (those who do survive)
And sold to colonial planters as soon as they arrive
The ships are then scrubbed thoroughly to kill the stench of death
And reloaded with consumables, rum, sugar and molasses

If not to the Caribbean then Virginia they went
Slaves traded there for cash goods tobacco, cotton and hemp
Before sailing back to Britain journeying at full steam
In the warm north easterly climate of the Atlantic Gulf Stream

But slave trading is problematic due to the nature of the beast
Ships arrive when goods are not ready or the expected load decreased
Unpredictable weather meant sail times would fluctuate
So Merchant ships returned half full and often very late

Hence Merchant fleets were often prepared and ordered just to go
And pick up only cash crops and manufactured cargo
Thus by-passing the African continent for shipment of the slaves
To focus attention on delayed stock so deliveries could be made

Jamaica is the trading hub on the middle passage route
Where plantation life is hellish, slave masters absolute brutes
Jamaican slaves start to murmur if only they could stray
Off the island onto these ships and gladly sail away

Once they reached England things would not be so rough
Cos rumour had it, on the mainland life simply was not tough
Two slaves in 1772 managed to execute their plan
To smuggle themselves on board a ship headed for the motherland.

2

CHAPTER I

This is a tale of a sibling twin
Her brother strong and tall, she lean and thin
Born among slaves in Jamaica
Of a woman cruelly shipped from Africa
The siblings managed to fulfil a dream
To escape the island and the colonial regime
On a Merchant ship carrying goods for trade
But with no legal pass no money they made
Instead as stowaways
They lay
Quiet as a mouse
In their makeshift boat house
For days and days, nights and nights, months and months...

They just about coped with conditions poor
The raging seas causing storms to roar
The rats, the mites
Other things that bite
Feeding on scraps the odd bit of port
Sneaking around trying not to be caught
As nearing death, fate in God's hand
They craftily managed their survival
Courageously hung on until their arrival
In this here Bristol Port England

The weather was cold, no shoes on their feet no money in their pocket
to spend
The desperate souls had taken a chance as surely now life would end

SHELAAGH

They banged on doors looking for work all too often the reply was,
    'No!'
They suffered insults, beatings and abuse but kept going cos their minds
    said, 'Go!'
They kept up their spirits by dancing at night to the sound of nature's
    song
The howling of the wind, the cry of the beasts provided the basic drum
And when they danced they were as happy as punch
Their troubles left behind wrapped up in a bunch
They felt like king and queen of the land
Entertaining themselves barefoot in the sand

They had a talent unbeknown to them
That was spotted one day by a businessman
He owned a tavern in City Square
But business was not thriving there

The struggling proprietor espied them while walking through a storm
He hid behind the bushes to witness the duo perform
His brain went, 'Tick, tick! There's money to be had
With an act!' He thought, 'business is bad
The Negress girl is a fascinating thing
I'm not altogether sure about him
But an act starring her my punters will grow
There's no time to lose', thought the impresario
'I'll offer a fair price to take her with me
I'll train her to perform on a stage and she'll be
All the rage in my pub in the City'

He approached them stealthily lest they should show fear then with a
     polite cough
He got their attention and with a friendly smile gave them a chance to
     show off
So mesmerized was he by the girl's twists and turns
He gives a coin to her brother tells him the terms
But La Petite on seeing grows extremely cross
'Now listen Sah who say him 'ere were boss?'
Stunned -
Her brother pulls her aside
Looks his sister in the eye
Orders her to keep quiet and play dumb
But La Petite is not prepared to stand and twiddle her thumb
Directly in defiance of him
She immediately decides to muscle in

'Now Sah what you do and what 'ya want?'
The man appears nonchalant
As he moves his umbrella to shelter her from the rain
Her brother quickly tries to explain
'Him like the way you dance you see
Him want you t' go dance in the Big City'
'Me? And what about you?' she says
Her brother sadly shakes his head

La Petite does not like the sound of his plan
Turns her face looks sternly at the man

'Now listen if you want me to dance fi you
You'll have to take mi brodah too'

SHELAAGH

Her furious brother begins to feel
His sister is about to blow the deal
'What are you doing Sis playing da fool?
What the hell is wrong wid you?
Dis is your chance for some security'
'Wherever I go', she says, 'yah coming wid me'

She boldly strides back to the man
To bargain terms as best she can

'Whatever it is you offering
You have to take me and him
We want dis much money', she holds up 8 fingers
The man of affaires shakes his head and counters
She continues to argue the amount of pay
'Til the proprietor shakes his head and walks away
Her exasperated brother quickly runs after him
Says they will accept whatever he is offering

He agrees he will take the two of them
But the pay he offers is a paltry sum
His sister bargains water and bread
And a place for them both to each rest their head

The final deal is struck in due course
And the two are soon in a cart and horse
Travelling in style along the shore
From Bristol port where they were poor
To London town
The home of the man

And soon to become their own

With a job to earn money and a bolthole to stay
The sibling's troubles were wafted away
No more dancing for trees
The wind and the breeze
But for rowdy gents
In his establishment

The entrepreneur with no time to spare
Got to work on fashioning the pair
He could not dance and could not sing
Yet he would sit on a stool... Tah... Tah...Tah...ring!
And cracking his whip on the floor
As he shouted and yelled out for, 'More!'
Tapping and stamping his massive feet
(Usually out of time with the beat
Which drove the pair completely nuts
But they contained their frustration in their guts)
They watched the man getting carried away
Passionately allowing his body to sway
Backwards and forth as he rattled his tambourine
This way they cobbled together a routine
With her brother on drums and violin
And La Petite dancing doing her own thing

In a few days the owner was promoting and advertising
Something more exciting than the usual cock fighting
He proudly introduced to the tiny stage
His newly found drummer and dancing maid

SHELAAGH

Night after night they performed in the town
Soon word of the two got around
Though the pub remained dingy and rather grim
A more sophisticated crowd began sneaking in
People from the rich aristocracy
Dashing young knights and old dignitaries
Were filling the aisles
Some who had travelled for miles
To drink gin galore
And come and adore
The act named, "Bo Peeps and Jangles"

In no time the books at "The Chequered Jack"
Were out of the red and in the black
But despite the money the house was making
The duo did not benefit from the takings
However, as popularity and profits grew
A transformed proprietor came into view
Expensively dressed in flamboyant attire
Welcoming the regulars in his mini Empire

Curiously, every night in the very same chair
Sat one particular Frenchman there
He was round and stout
Looked like he had gout
And his face was ruby red

His eyes stared wide at the petite Negress and the rhythms of her twists
        and turns
He wanted badly to touch her skin to caress her neat and little bones

8

But all he could do was watch the charade
And give handsome applause for the petite maid

After a while La Petite
Noticed the man in his seat
And with kind spirit found a moment to wave at monsieur
During the pas de deux

The man was delighted
Got obsessed and excited
And while drinking port
Thought and thought
Of a way to engage
With this girl onstage

He would sneak backstage during the show
Leave an anonymous gift with instructions on where she must go
For them to meet
In the street

He will not write words but draw pictures instead
As questionable if she would understand what she read
But he will make it clear to her not to forget
Their tête à tête must be kept secret

Then came the night to put plan into action, he sat in his usual seat
Suspecting nothing La Petite clocks him once while dancing on her feet
But as if by magic when she came to wave the man had mysteriously
    gone
A slight look of concern then composure resumed she continues to
    carry on

SHELAAGH

The applause is raging as they finish their scene
She quickly dashes behind a screen
There hidden behind the door
A small trinket box sits on the floor
She stares hard at the box and the note beside
Addressed to 'La Négresse Petite' - O my!

Fool, she thinks not wishing to touch the exquisite new box near her
     hand
'This can't be for me, its beauty too great, this handsome gift is far too
     grand'

But she looks around, there is no one there so who else could there be
She opens the door takes one more peep, to see if there is someone to
     see

The large man on the other side of the door is pressed up flat against
     the wall
So La Petite's wandering eye does not notice him at all

Now she thinks she is alone her courage grows her arm stretches out to
     hold -
But she instead with one finger only gently strokes the box made of solid
     gold

Gradually her fingers begin to wrap the delicate treasure
Enjoying the pleasure
She tightens her grip and ever so slow
Lifts the box towards her face which now begins to glow

But the biggest prize is still to come, she wonders what could be inside...
As she raises her thumb to open the lid
A sudden gasp as she catches a glimpse of the round red face of the fella
    hid
A finger pressed tight on his lip

The frightened girl almost loses her grip
And nearly drops
The delicate box
Composure resumed she puts it back in its place
Clearly wrong for the expression on his face
Tells her, the thing that is sealed
He wants revealed
And without any chat
She does just that

Carefully with little doubt she opens the lid
To see what is hid
- inside
Eyes open wide
And light up to see
The wonderful delicacy
A special treat
Delicious and sweet
Excitement trickles down to her feet

Having stared hard, she gently utters
C h o c o l a t e! She mutters
She could hardly say
Only a dream could bring this her way
She looks at the man a tear in her eye he gestures for her to eat

SHELAAGH

The sweetmeat
She hesitates then takes a bite
He watches, she savours, he delights at the sight
Then beckons her to follow him into the night

'O no!' she thinks she begins to scare
'This dream may be the start of an awful nightmare
Me? Him? Meet?
Outside in di street?
Why does a man of his class
Dare ask?
A dignitary and a girl like me
A scandal can't he see it would be
– at best? And what is more for sure
Dem outside will think me a bleedin' whore!
No! I really can't... Well maybe I can
I'll walk 10 paces behind the man
No this is absurd the man is mad
This is bad
Must find an excuse
– Quick! Mi head hurts... mi toes sore... mi bowels a bit loose...'

She thought of everything to make him go
But really she did not have the heart to say no
Curiosity had got the better of she
Who could this man really be?
Seduced by such flattery
Not to mention
The special attention

'Just a minute - I'll just get mi cloak', said she
'Please wait for me
- Outside there'
Concealing her fear
Points to the door at the rear
A nod of his head
Meant he heard what she said
With a curled up smile almost skipping inside
He puts on his hat
Gives it a quick tap
And dashes to the street out back

La Petite, having stalled a little and stalled some more
Grabs her sack and shawl
Walks tentatively towards to door
Then hesitates... she turns away
Still not sure whether to go or stay
After a while, a sudden and hurried rap at the door makes her jump –

She waits a beat -

'Négresse', she hears, 'Négresse my sweet
Come quickly, quickly, vite! vite!'

The dear soul
Through the keyhole
With her eye
Thinks to espy
The man again

'What d' ya want with me really sir?' she softly cries

SHELAAGH

The calming voice outside replies
'No need to be afraid
Dear maid
I have something of interest I want you to see
Please come with me'

Now in that moment without much thought
As to whether she is feeling calm or distraught
An inner excitement begins to flow
And so the decision is made to go

As the Negress steps outside the gentleman of old
Offers his arm for her to hold

'Monsieur', she says quite bold
'I do not wish to be impolite
But I do not think that it is right
For you to be seen to be
So familiar with me'

'Ridiculous!' he says, 'What do you mean
To be seen
To be so familiar? Child
Methinks I understand your pride
But you should trust my integrity my dear
Have no fear
Take my arm
I promise I do not mean you harm'

The older man's honest words of kind

Does little to alleviate the state of concern in her mind
'Twas not his integrity of which she had doubt
Instead the whole class, race, status thing 'twas what it was about
However, not wishing to provoke a scene
She places her arm in between
His but not before
She was sure
Her shawl was raised high on top her head
And across her face near covering her eyes
As in a disguise

Surprised the older man looks at her bemused
And amused
He chuckles, 'Does this make you feel better?'

'Please do not mock my face
I do not wish to be disgraced
So do not mock for it is clear
You do not understand my fear'

Not wishing to cause more offence
In his defence
The older man grows silent

And in a fashion most discrete
He leads her down the cobbled street

They eventually arrive at The Crown and Bell
Which one should note was a stylish hotel of sorts
And of this Inn someone once wrote:

SHELAAGH

"The Crown and Bell with rooms so fine
Is a favoured choice of the fashionable set of our time
Furnishings in rooms are chosen with care
And those who dine eat with silverware"

But La Petite did not need a review
To formulate her own personal view
Of the place
Staring her in the face
With ladies inside dressed in lace
Prim, proper and pale-faced
Sitting alongside their elegant gents
Talking and gossiping in the hoity-toity sense
She did not need a review
For her gut instinct knew
This is not the sort of dwelling
They should both go in
Should they both enter there
The guests, the Inn keeper would start to stare
Making La Poor Petite
Feel like an absolute freak

And as they near approached the door
La Petite doth start to protest once more

'Is this where you live monsieur?'
'I have lodgings here it's true, I do'
'Well that is good for you
As one thing is for sure
I will not be walking through that door'

'Come, stop your protests you charming thing
Your negative chants have a tiresome ring
The people inside are quite polite
You will not have trouble here tonight
I've made my intentions plain and clear
Besides the surprise I have for you is in here'

Now with rage and anger she screams
'You arrogant person of means
You unscrupulous and insensitive man
This surely is your plan
To get yourself laid
By this exotic poor maid
In your specially chosen Inn
For you to commit your sin
Don't take me for a fool you evil cat
Cos I know where your head is at'

And with these words she runs off down the track
Leaving him calling for her to, 'Come back!'

The man, now frustrated and angry
More with himself than with she
Starts running after her down the street
But the little maid is quick on her feet
Soon he is forced to accept defeat
As he loses sight of her

The dejected, rejected man
Will have to think of another plan.

CHAPTER II

Weeks had passed and not a word
Had La Petite heard
From the strange man
And neither had he time to go
To the show
Where once he had a regular seat
To watch her moving to the beat
The man she had met in cloak and vest
Had clearly gone and lost interest

Furthermore the situation at
The Chequered Jack
Was changing as time went by
Why?
The proprietor these days did not seem to care
He was hardly ever there
Once the novelty wore off and he had become rich
He seemed to lose interest and left the pitch
Of the happily thriving gin mill
The place once again was going downhill

Aside from work life was quite bland
For La Petite - On the other hand
Things were truly at their best
In her brother's love nest...

Since born the same day one might think them alike
But brother and sister were not the same type

SHELAAGH

While he was tall, she was short
He drank much, she drank naught
He well-built dapper, gregarious, dudish
She sort of slender, unsociable, prudish
'Though she very bright and he more dim
She wished she could be more like him
But rather risk meeting with lowlifes and whores
She chose to stay night after night indoors
And finish off her nightly chores

So strange when the Frenchman made a pass
None was more surprised than she
That she did go along with he
But less now more surprised are we
That she did blow the opportunity
Of his approach
With her reproach
Knowing what we know now
Of how
She is a fair maid lacking in adventure
So back to her brother's nightly venture

While La Petite was left alone
To ponder and wonder on her own
Her younger, more sociable fraternal twin
Would make off down to the Jamaica Inn...

The Jamaica Inn, in Blackfriars on Main Street
Was the pub where black folk could meet
To catch up on the daily news

And formulate their own views
On current affairs, and other issues
Such as slavery and the misuse
Of house labour were things often debated
Some discussions got very animated
While eating stews and drinking rum
Singing and dancing they had become
Raucous, rowdy lively and gay
Before crashing out and back to work the next day

Here in this pub Jangles whose real name, by the way, was Bo
But for the purposes of the show
Was known as Jangles, likewise Bo Peeps was the stage name
Just the same
For La Petite whose real name was Violet

Here in this pub Bo had met
A pretty dark maid he could hardly forget
With full round figure large innocent eyes
Plump dark brown lips, strong solid thighs
Her plaited hair kept neat and tidy
He would see her every Friday
Ask his sister to help him prepare
For this meet she would trim his hair
Bo would shine up his shoes as best he could
In the hope of impressing Miss Ruby Greenwood

Ruby was a house servant to the family
Of The Right Honourable George Kennedy
A lawyer and politician
Not left nor right, a liberal Man

SHELAAGH

Famous for being outspoken
On particular topics especially
The outrage and injustice of slavery
He truly felt should be abolished
And slave ships demolished
This did not stop he and his spouse
Keeping servants in his house
Though firm as Master, he seemed to care
And Ruby Greenwood was happy there

Ruby had captured Bo's heart one night
When he and a friend caught sight
Of her looking innocent and shy
She smiled at him as she caught his eye
With confidence and gallant style he moved in quick
To savour her sweet aroma of oranges, thyme and garlic
(Due to the fact she worked much of her days in the kitchen)
No matter, for him a sweeter smell there could not have been

For many weeks he would make her laugh and try to sneak a little kiss
Though she felt very fond of him she had the strong will to resist
Soon they had reached a stage that they were doing more than talking
They were actually now courting
Sometimes seemingly cavorting

So the thing on Bo's mind he wanted to do
Was show his sweet love his love was true
Buy a ring
Do the proper thing
Ask her master if they could be

Bound in wedlock for eternity
Simply a case of saving enough money
To make an honest woman of his honey

So a promise to himself he made
That whenever he was paid
He would take three coins out from his pouch and pull them aside
To hide
In a tin
In the Spartan room he and his sister lived in

The darkened room measured five by four
He searched along the wooden floor
Carefully with a candlelight
Found out of immediate sight
A rat eaten hole that looked perfectly fine
Quickly he wastes no time
He wraps the coins in an old coloured neckerchief
Because of his belief
If put straight in
The tin
The coins would make a rattling sound
When knocked by rats scurrying around
Then he closed the lid and buried away
The premier savings of his nightly pay
And covered up the spot
With a simple copper chamber pot

For many weeks it became habitual
To carry out this banking ritual
Until his sister and lifelong saviour

SHELAAGH

Became inquisitive of his strange behaviour

Still as a mouse and with hawk's eyes
She spies
Bo one day
Counting the savings from his nightly pay
Having discovered the hidden spot
She contemplates pinching the whole darn lot
Then decides not to do
For fear of being beaten black and blue
Believing the money would be hers anyway
On his return prefers to say

'I found the money my dear
Have you got enough to get us outta here?
You know each night I dance in pain
Because of the cold wind and rain
My bones can barely take the strain
I bet you feel the same...'

Her nagging tones go on and on
'Enough', he says, 'of this sad song'
He allows himself to confess
The situation between he and his mistress

When Violet discovers the money is for a ring
She wastes no time in attacking him

'A ring! A ring! Money to buy a ring!
When you leave me near starving

When I am forced to beg on the street
For shoes to put 'pon my feet
Marriage! Where would that leave me?
Marriage! Never! I will not allow thee
Or the love that you have sown
To leave me abandoned on my own
Never!'

Furious as ever
She reaches for the box tosses it hard against the wall
A showering of coins begins to fall
Her brother quickly retaliates
Determined her neck he'll break
Grabs it with one strong arm
And more to her alarm
Lifts her body right off the floor
And hurls her through the open door

'A sad lonely spinster you'll remain', he cries
'Unwilling to live life and socialize
But no sister of mine will ever suppress
My chance to seal my happiness'

Furiously he gathers the coins that fell
Puts them in his pouch and leaves their cell

He wanders around for a while with one thing playing on his mind
What will he find
In terms of a simple wedding band
With the money he has to hand?

SHELAAGH

Eventually he stumbles upon a Jeweller's shop
Comes to the sudden stop
Eyes transfixed on the glistening bling
A voice behind startles him, 'You like that thing?'

He turns around
To face the direction of the sound
The round red face of the Frenchman stares
'Mi nat a t'ief', Bo quickly declares

The man looks warmly into his eyes
'It was not my intention to accuse you', he replies
'I understand the paranoia mind you
For I too am a foreigner - and a Jew!'
Chuckles spark with this little joke
Instantly the ice is broke

The proprietor of the shop invites Bo in
Bo's face is consumed by a massive grin
With head held high and shoulders back
He takes on the proud manner of an aristocrat
As he walks beside the owner who is shuffling along
As the conversation continues on
But the gentleman is more guarded in his tone
Once they are inside alone

'Forgive me but I know your face
I've seen you dancing in that place
With the Négresse girl - your wife perhaps?' He enquires the history

'No Sir mi sister, dat's the story'
Eyes of the man light up in glory

'And where is her husband, I presume she has one'
'No sir in fact she has none'

'I see', says the man
Trying as best as he can
Not to give too much away
In what he had to say
'So what brings you hunting jewel and pearl?'
'I seek something special for mi gal'
Bo says as he casts his eyes on a selection of plain gold posy rings
'How much the cheapest?' The man inspects – '10 shillings'

Bo peeps into his pouch not nearly enough
Cash to consider buying that sort of stuff
His disappointment he could not conceal
The Jeweller begins to feel
Compassion for the man
Offers him the best deal he can
He shows him a very simple band
Nothing grand
Not made of pure gold but that looked very nice
Tells him he can have it at a special price
On the condition that he persuades his sister to meet with him
That night at... he thinks for a moment then says... 'The Copthorn Inn'

Now the Copthorn Inn was a charming but much more
Downmarket place than the one tried before
It was written of this Inn in the weekly gazette:

27

SHELAAGH

"The Copthorn can be a lively sight
With people drinking throughout the night
If money is flowing whatever your race
They'll welcome you kindly into this place"

The older gent quickly figured in his head
The Négresse here would be less intimidated
But time alone would only tell
If his predictions worked out well

Bo cannot believe his luck
Immediately a deal seems struck
He holds out his hand to shake
The shopkeeper in turn reciprocates
Bo is about to hurry off
When he is stopped by the man's cough

The owner walks towards him once more
And gently closes the half opened door
'As a businessman I'm sure you can appreciate
In order for you to secure the rate
A small deposit you'll have to pay'
'I hear', says Bo, 'how much today?'
'For now the money lodged in your sack
More when you come back'

They take an account
Of the amount
- Nine halfpennies and two farthings
'If you pay the same amount each week

In six months' time it's yours to keep'
Bo's face suddenly drops slowly to the ground
As reality sinks in of the money to be found
Nine halfpennies had taken weeks to save
The ring won't be his 'til a yearlong age
He looks at the man in a desperate way
Then dares to say

'What is my sister worth to you?
I mean... is this the best deal you can do?'
'You mean,' says the merchant, 'you would sell your sister for the price
    of a ring
Am I up for that sort of thing?'

The man watches as Bo's face
Drops further down in deep disgrace

'No need to be embarrassed by it
I understand all too well your hardship
Your sister means a lot to me but not in the way you think
Here have a drink'

He places two silver goblets on top the counter
Pours out wine from a crystal decanter

'I am a jeweller, an artist with an artist's bowl
I wish to feed the creative soul
With your sister acting as my muse...'

Bo looks at him confused

SHELAAGH

'...I do not expect you to comprehend
Simply send
Your sister to me before the cock crows twice
And I will reconsider the price
Cannot say fairer than that with regards the ring
But there is one more thing
With this knowledge in your possession
I trust I will have your discretion?'

'No worry', says Bo, 'I will not say a word
Of what I've heard
I assure you thank you kindly Sir
Tonight you will meet my good sister'

The man raises his glass and takes a swig
Bo picks up his glass and knocks back his
The man lifts up the latch to open the door
Bo without hesitation leaves the store.

CHAPTER III

It is evening time in London Town
The city streets have quietened down
Pavements beaten down with rain
Violet and Bo in the pub again
Entertaining pickled patrons benched
Others entering utterly drenched
Stamp their feet, shake themselves off
Before settling at the drinking trough

That night after the show desists
Bo turns to Violet and insists
'Tonight you come wid me mi gal
So grab your t'ings and meet mi pal'

Violet surprised
Replies
'Have you gone mad in da head?
What kind of nonsense is that y' said?'

Bo unappreciative of her words
Strides up to her, grabs her shoulders
From behind shouts down her ear
'Are you deaf my dear!
Is there something you didn't hear!'

'Ahhhh! Stop it! Stop it!' she screams, 'What is wrong with you?'
He says, 'just do what I tell you to do'
'I will not,' Violet screams defiantly

SHELAAGH

Bo stares at her she stares back at he

He shouts, 'No ifs, buts, what, when, which way, maybe!
You will come with me however, I declare
Even if I have to drag you kicking and screaming by the hair'

When done Bo throws her over his shoulder
Violet's legs kicking frantically, she is screaming over and over
'Bo let me be!'
As she tries to bite her way free

Outside in the street Bo's big strong hands grip tight
As he drags his sister a quarter of a mile in the night
Towards the bustling Copthorn Inn
Where the man is said to be seated within

The pub is crowded he pushes open the door
It is hard to circulate the floor
They weave their way through the massive place
Bo checking every single man's face

Finally he recognises
The profile of the Jeweller he lionises
Sitting rather hunched on a bench
Being served up food by a buxom wench
On the table in front of him just to the side
A box measuring eight inches by one foot wide

The flat box is made of brown velvet
The Jeweller's left hand seems glued to it

The round red face looks up at them
Suddenly shock her recollection
Can't fathom out how Bo and he made the connection

'My sister as you requested
Please don't forget the money invested'
Bo drops her down in front of him
Then makes on out for the Jamaica Inn

'Don't leave me!' She screams
Bo ignores the scene
'I'll get you for this my brother - you traitor!'
The Jeweller begs her, 'calm down deal with him later'

Her angry eyes look hard at him then notice the box lying on the table
Trying to get her emotions stable
She asks, 'What's inside the box?
More chocolates?' she mocks

He does not answer suffice to say, 'vous-avez faim chérie?' (Are you
    hungry dear?)
She nods. The Jeweller offers her the rest of his plate and a pint of beer
She quickly demolishes the lot without chatter
Picks up the dish licks the platter
Then with her hand without much grace
Crudely wipes dripping grease off her face
Then asks again, 'What's in the case?'

'Not here', he says, 'come follow me'
Impatient of the mystery
She looks at him mistrusting unsure

SHELAAGH

'Look', he says, 'have I hurt you before?'
'No', she admits, 'not yet'- her bitter tone
'But you are a man and I am here alone'
'So as a man', he says, 'may I not be an honourable gent?'
'As a woman', she replies, 'Mi nah trust no man's intent'
'But you would like to see what's inside the box, I trust?'
'Yes but...' he interrupts, 'then trust me you must
– Come!'

The box is placed under his arm
Persuaded by his manly charm
She follows him pushing through the crowded room
Until they reach a wooden door at the back of the saloon
That led to a darkened corridor
With a stone cold paving floor

He picks up a lantern hanging in front of him
Leads her to the foot of some wooden stairs so grim
Their feet venture up the narrow stairs in the place
The 'clunk! clunk!' hollow sound makes her heart race

At the top and to her right
The door of the room where she is set to spend the night
He gives her the lantern for him to see
Whilst hunting around his person for the key

The big iron key he hides in his sock
Which he uses to unlock the lock

They enter the room it is dark and cold

She wonders whether she has been sold
Outright to the man. She begins to shiver
He senses her quiver
Quickly hands her a blanket to wrap round herself
Places the lantern on the mantelshelf
Lights the fire below
She is mesmerized by the golden glow
Candles on the walls he proceeds to light
To make the room seem a little more bright
Now she can see the dark furniture in there
A simple bed, a writing desk and a wooden chair

The Jeweller places the box on top the desk pulls up the chair
The girl's eyes still transfixed on the fire, continue to stare

He calls to her as he takes his seat
Slowly she moves to stand by his feet
He looks at her face
As he raises the lid of the velvet case
Her careful examination
Eyes consumed with fascination

Inside and between the satin lined sheets
A host of beautiful colourful sweets
Of all shapes and size
Are what are in front of her very eyes
The sweets are laid out in rows
She brings down her nose
To smell
One made of caramel

SHELAAGH

But all is not well
As far as she can tell

She reaches out
And pops one into her mouth
To see if she could work out the twist
Immediately feels a slap across her wrist
'Ouch!'

'Non!' he says looking sternly at her
The sweet tumbles from the hand of the girl
He reacts double quick to catch the stone holds it gently to the
    candlelight
The sparkling gem an impressive sight

'These treats
Are not sweets
For you to eat
They are precious stones
To decorate your delicate bones'
He goes on to give her an education
Via his detailed explanation

'Rubies you see
Bright as a red cherry
It is said if worn by yourself
Will ward off misfortune and ill health'

'Where they do come from Africa?' 'No Burmese
If you please

If Africa's what you desire
The word Topaz actually means fire
These are they with tones so mellow
In sherry, pink, blue, green and yellow'

She picks up something vibrant and green
'Emeralds', he says, 'aren't they supreme?'
Eyes light up as he gives one to her
'The finest in the world from Columbia'

She puts it back points to another
Tinted stone sitting under the cover
'Sapphires saved from the matrix of Kashmir
See the lustre's exceptionally clear
The most valuable one for you
Is this one here in cornflower blue'

He gives it to her to hold for a little while
Then takes it back puts it in the box with style

'Or perhaps my inquisitive little girl
You'd prefer
The exquisite charm of the River pearl
Tears of the gods from the sea
Displaying such magnificent beauty'

'Where they do come from?' she asks the man
'From the shells of the oyster fish in Japan'

Having presented the gamut of gems

SHELAAGH

Explaining the qualities of all of them
Her eyelids now beginning to drop
When he takes one final gem out from the lot
She views the colourless gem and is hypnotised
By the pure fire and lustre in front of her eyes

'Diamonds from Brazil ma petite Négresse
Are the most precious jewel any girl could possess'
She moves in gradually to touch
But sharply the gem is pull back from her and the box shut

'C'est tout! ma chérie que j'adore
Tomorrow I will show you more'

He moves towards the door, 'You may stay here tonight
But leave through the window before daylight'
'I'm scared monsieur', she calls out, 'wait!'
'I must go now', he says, 'it is late'

He grabs the box without saying a thing
Leaves the room and locks her in

Violet rushes bangs hard on the door
'Let me out! Let me out! Please sir! Monsieur!'

There is no response to her cries
Tears well up in her eyes
As she continues to pound the door
Until her exhausted hand can pound no more
Finally she is forced to give in to the fact

38

There is no way this man is coming back

Her back rests against the door
Then slumps slowly to the floor
In a state of shock she tries to hold back the tears
In all these years
It is the first time she has been on her own
Away from her humble home
And her once dependable brother
Having now seemingly betrayed her

Eventually the bed looks tempting -

Violet goes up to it
Removes the blanket
But chooses instead
To rest her weary head
On the floor
Curled up like a ball
A strange thing it may seem, to do
But this is what she was used to

Meanwhile, the centre of attention at the Jamaica Inn
Are a drunken Bo and his girl starting to sing
And entertain the regular folks
With music, dancing and dirty jokes

Outside in the street
The night watchmen on the beat
Can hear the sound of the loud
Joyous, raucous crowd

SHELAAGH

But cannot join the hive
Of total bedlam inside
For this establishment be
Only for black folk you see
Those with colour white of skin
Are not permitted to participate within

'Tis true at this time even this segregation
Was practised within the population

Inside, Bo intent on impressing his mistress
Decides to show off his musical prowess
By picking up the French horn
And playing it expertly 'til dawn

When finished with the band
He leads his girl out by the hand
The two of them worse for wear
However, they do not seem to care
Giggling and tripping over
Desperately trying to act sober
In an attempt to avoid arrest
Tonight they are very blessed
The beat cops freely let them go
For others though this is not so

In the background we see
Poor souls who were not so lucky
We watch and hear them cry
As more watchmen standing by

Pull others aside and wait to haul in
Their friends and companions exiting
The pub's main doors -
Suddenly a tranquil pause

Bo places his arm around his girl
Gently strokes a plaited curl

Then standing by a railing
Emotions unveiling
He doth profess his true love to Ruby
Then I must confess romantically
They walk together to the nearest park
A kiss and a cuddle they have in the dark

Bo's body begins to crave her
She unable to control her behaviour
Normally she would say she wouldn't
Knowing now he really shouldn't
For the first time this very night
Sensing no one to be around
Their bodies lay relaxed upon the ground
Then in urgent and poetic fashion
They let themselves give in to passion

In contrast, Violet on the floor lays rigid beneath the blanket
Struggling to get a good night's kip
The ever present noise of the cockroaches
Surround her as midnight soon approaches
Confused and frightened she tries to sleep
But all she can do is weep and weep.

CHAPTER IV

The following day when daylight breaks
Violet's eyes fixate
On the narrow and small
Window inserted in the wall
She reflects for a moment on the man she once feared
Who seems less frightening now but a little weird

'Why pass,' she thinks, 'on the opportunity to make
A pass, an advance, possibly rape
But instead choose to provide a means of escape?'
She ponders the meaning of the text
Her mind fast forwards to what's in store next?

She visualises a typical day
Begging in the streets the usual way
Among busy crowds with her brother
Cap in one hand begging bowl in the other
Pestering citizens passing by
Together they act out a lie
An unethical survival game
Where one plays blind and the other lame
Winning hearts and sympathy
From liberal folk with money
And naturally able to give
To the desperate poor who live
Without a trace of wealth
In abject poverty and ill health

SHELAAGH

She tidies herself a bit
Then makes her way towards her exit
The sound of burning embers crackling
She takes a peek outside - nothing much happening

She begins to examine her means of escape
Easy enough she thinks to make

Beneath the ledge
Near the edge
She spots a ridge in the wall
Where her foot should hold so she doesn't fall
The next challenge should excite
Sliding herself down the pipe
To the top of the railing
Should be plain sailing
Then the final jump
Should not cause a nasty bump

She spends a moment gazing out the window pane
Before opening the window then shutting it again

Outside the quiet street comes to life at last
People on horses trotting pass
Footmen assisting gentle ladies
Mothers wrestling with their babies

Footsteps rushing to and fro
Market traders on the go
A crescendo of pitter patter

Fuses the blend of chitter chatter
Emerging through the cloud of noise
The effervescent voice of the 12-year old paper boys
Ringing their bell
While shouting out the daily news to sell

'Read all about it! "The Somerset Case!"'

Seen weaving through the crowd in haste
The Jeweller with his cane and a sack
Stops briefly by the paper stack
Exchanges a coin for The Gazette
No time to read it properly yet
Only the front page headliner is scanned on the journal bought

It reads: "SOMERSET CASE TO BE REFERRED TO THE KINGS
    COURT"

Precisely what it read:
"Yefterday Lord Mansfield, Chief Juftice faid
The cafe of Somerfet the Negro will be referred
To the Court of the Kings Bench to be heard
A fignificant cafe in history
Set to challenge the legality of flavery
For true
In the faid year of 1772"

He places the paper under his arm with the cane
Before racing down the street again

SHELAAGH

He is out of breath when he reaches the Inn
Thudding his way up the stairs huffing and puffing

He turns the lock to his room in panic
As he can't seem to catch his breath and is manic
Coughing and wheezing, making an awful din
Like his life is about to cave in

He enters the room drops the sack by the bed
Then collapses onto it half dead
The newspaper tumbles from beneath his arm
As he takes a moment to get himself calm

When his pulse has decreased to normal rate
Head adopted a more tranquil state
Heartbeat stopped going berserk
He settles down to get to work

He moves himself to the chair stretches out his limb
And slowly drags the bag towards him
Pulls out from the sack
A candlestick and a small pack
Of flints and steel to strike up a light
In order to enhance his sight

Then he gets out a large book bound with leather
Undoes the ties which hold it together
Layers of parchment sit beneath
The cover that is decorated with gold leaf

Next he removes a wooden box
Containing some small ink pots
Feather quills
And money bills

He removes the tops
From the pots
Places them neatly in a row
All prepared and ready to go
He opens a blank page in the book
Pauses a moment to have a look

Gradually his body takes on a new guise
The Master's obsession displayed in his eyes
The craftsman's passion possessing him
Provides a platform for him to begin

He conjures up a large collection
Of glimmering ideas for selection
Corsage brooches, diamond rings
Necklaces, bracelets many things

The creative eye begins to scan
The options for his jewelled plan
A rainbow of gems swirl in his mind's light
Seductively tempting like sirens at night

His brow moist with perspiration
A sudden burst of inspiration
He picks up a feathered pen
In his head he counts to ten

SHELAAGH

Allowing time for his brain to think
Before dipping his quill in the ink

Without wasting time
He starts with a simple outline
Executes his vision
With neat precision
Etching sketching transforming the pallor
With intricate detailed droplets of colour

The process sends him into a trance
As he lets the artist's quill just dance
Erotic beauty turns stomach to jelly
Artistic fuel dragged from his belly
Heart and soul are so submerged
He doesn't notice Violet emerge
At the height of his meditation
Her sudden voice breaks his concentration

'What are you doing?'

The man so startled, taken aback
Nearly has a heart attack
Furious he is been caught off guard
He raises his stick as if to cane her hard
Lets out a supreme primal scream, 'AAAh!!
You were there all the time you said nothing!' He did cry
'Was frightened heard you wheezing Sir, thought you would die'

He shouts at her

LA PETITE NEGRESS

'You disobedient girl
Didn't I tell you to leave?'
'But sir, I do not know what it is you want of me'

He bangs his cane firmly on the floor
La Petite recoils from him once more
'Must I train you', he says, 'like an animal child?
Must I treat you like something wild?'

She backs herself against the wall
Cowers down into a ball
'No sir, don't beat me, I beg of you
Whatever you want me to do I'll do'

She grabs the neckline of her cotton dress
Pulls down hard to reveal her breast...

Stunned! The Jeweller hastily applies
One hand to his face to cover his eyes
In absolute and total shock
He quickly demands she does up her frock
For this, for sure, was not the kind
Of thing the man had on his mind

He apologises filled with guilt and shame
Gets a grip of himself and releases the cane
Then looks into her scared teary eyes
Offers her his sweaty handkerchief to wipe them dry

'I am not a cruel man I promise
Whatever plan I have for you is honest'

49

SHELAAGH

He stares hard focusing on her lips
Stretches out his quivering finger tips
Reaches out to touch her shoulder
Repeating, 'calme-toi, calme-toi', over and over

She is stood frozen, uneasy
Feeling somewhat queasy
As his fingers move to check
The sleek contours of her slender neck

'Ah', he says to himself, 'perfectly chic'
Mumbling under his breath, 'magnifique'

He hunts about his person for a coin to proffer
She looks at him suspiciously but is tempted by the offer
'Sir, you may be a respectable and generous man
But I do not wish to be made into a courtesan'

'I understand your will and I will keep my promise to thee
But take this money and you must promise me...
To return here tonight my friend, do you understand?'
She pauses nods her head before snatching the coin from his hand

'Now my dear you must go'
She heads to the small window
'Not there child! For now it is day
You best leave through the doorway'

She quickly applies the brake

Correcting her innocent mistake

Then leaves the room with a look of concern

Contemplating whether or not she will return.

CHAPTER V

That afternoon and keen to receive some pay
Bo hunts for Violet who has been away all day
And is now wandering the street
Near the homes of the elite

Along a footpath where she arrived unbidden
She spots something of interest tucked away hidden
Old clothes rich folk have dumped in a heap
Violet rushes over to the mound and digs deep

Much of the stuff was worse for wear
Violet does not in the least bit care

She pulls out a wide brimmed fashionable hat
Sees a pheasant tail feather sticks it in that
Discovers a blue cape and man's checked shirt
Puts them on over her old woollen skirt
Finds odd shoes and socks strewn over the concrete
Uses the footwear to cover her bare feet
Saunters off smugly filled with delight
Despite the fact she looks quite a sight
Wearing one sock striped the other white
One shoe too big and the other too tight

She takes a moment to rest on a park seat
Famished, she has not had a thing to eat
Mentally she prepares for hunger and starvation
Having failed to carry out her begging occupation

SHELAAGH

Her pained expression all forlorn
Suddenly change and a smile is born
When she remembers as best she can
The generosity of the man

She hunts about her person and retrieves the half-Crown coin
Buried deep in her skirt pocket by her loin
Delight!

She gives it a quick bite
It is real alright
More money than she has ever earned in a night
She runs off with a hop and a skip
With the coin tightly in her grip

Grinning like a Cheshire cat
She dreams of sporting a fancy hat
A pair of sandals made for her feet
'I could go and buy some meat'
She thinks
'And tasty drinks
Or perhaps sack cloth to bind my hair
Savour the flavour of a roasted hare
Or juicy suckling pig
With apricots and a fig
Or even a pheasant
To give to a peasant...'

She gets carried away with thoughts not fit for the poor

LA PETITE NEGRESS

As she runs outside to catch the tail end of the market store

Amid the crowd this late time of day
Her brother is lurking not far away
And by chance catches a glimpse of her
Violet still possessed with delusions of grandeur
Continues to dream about extravagancies
But settles simply for some bread and cheese
Leaving her change at this stage
To be spent in another phase

'Violet' Bo calls out as she makes her selection
She turns round, sees him, runs in the other direction
'Come back woman!' He bellows loud and clear
She runs off faster pretending she cannot hear
Giggling and laughing fading out of sight
Clutching her goods and her money tight
It appears she is leading in the sibling fight

She halts at a spot she believes is safe
A quick "butchers" does not see Bo about the place

Tummy aching legs are sore
Can't stand the hunger pangs no more
Parks her tush
Behind a bush
Proudly claiming victory
Before settling down to eat her tea

But a determined Bo
Who has not let go

55

SHELAAGH

Freezes
When he spots her unwrapping the cheeses

Violet, totally unaware
Of her brother's presence there
Is about to take a bite
And satisfy her appetite
When Bo sneaks right up behind her
And grabs the parcel of food from under the girl
Violet screams hysterically
'NO! NO! Viper! Ginnal! Give it back to me!'

Bo does not, instead takes great pleasure
Devouring the whole stolen treasure
In front of her hungry eyes
Amidst her desperate cries
'Please Bo give some to me
Can't you see, I'm hungry'

Bo continues to gobble with glee
Showing not an ounce of mercy
Claiming back his victory
And leaving not a crumb in sight
For poor Violet to satisfy her appetite

'How could you Bo? How could you dare?'
'Come on sister, we're supposed to share'

His mocking retort makes her angry
She looks at him hard then foolishly

Says, 'I'll have the last laugh you see
Look here money just for me'

She holds up the remaining coins in her hand
Confidently gets up to stand
Bo eyes widen start to stare
'Where you get this?' 'Why you care?'
She says, quickly turning away from him
With the money protected inside her limb

Bo runs after her grabs her wrist
Immediately she clenches her fist
'Leave me! Leave me! Let me be!'
'Not before you tell me where you got da money'

Violet remains dumb
Bo pulls hard on her thumb
She holds her hand tight
Bo tries to prise it open she begins to bite
Crying, 'Leave me! Mi want shoes to put 'pon mi feet
Have mercy Bo, mi did not eat'

She struggles with him at length
But is overcome by his strength
The coins tumble to the ground
Bo is quick to scoop them up in his hand

'It is clear mi dear you've found
A new way of surviving in this land
So once again I ask of thee
How you come by this money?'

SHELAAGH

Violet sees his threatening eyes
Drops to the ground and just cries

'Violet!', Bo shouts, 'Are you listening to me?
How you get the money?'

Violet lacking the energy to fight
Finally says, 'The man you sold mi to last night'

'So what 'im expect you to do?'
'Nothing', she says,
'Nothing?' he replies, 'You must take me fi a fool
Why would a man like he give you money for free?
No man gives a poor woman like you such charity
I say, "Rewards!" for a night of copulation'

Violet outraged by this speculation
'Shut up brother how dare you be so crude'

'Sister dear you are not such a prude'

Violet grows more angry and hurt
At having to protest she got money without lifting her skirt

'When will you see him again?'
Bo wants her to explain

'Don't know, don't care'

Bo says, 'Sister, you must continue dis affair
You've found a way to earn us a living
Through this man and his generous giving
Go back to the man get me three more of these
Play your cards right and you'll have all the luxuries
Your heart can tend
My dear friend
Go back to him
Commit your sin
Think nothing of the act
If lying on your back can earn us a crust
Then lie on your back you must'

Violet outraged at the implication
That she should support her brother through fornication
Storms off stomping her feet on the ground
Wondering what is this life she has found

Bo rushes after her
Puts his arm around his sister
'You may think me kinda harsh mi gal
But this is about our survival'

His tone then softens -

'Look, if you really received this treasure
Without offering pleasure
Then truly you are blessed
A lucky gal I would suggest
Here, take back your coins and forget all the rest'

SHELAAGH

Violet takes back the coins, holds them up mockingly
And yells back at her brother the winning words, 'Victory!'

She is about to go on her way
When her brother has one more thing to say
'Sister seriously
You need to find a fellow who'll take care of thee'

'You dear brother' she says, 'will look after me'
'No girl. I've found love I will be happy'

His words hit home brutally hard
Violet cannot believe he is choosing to discard
Her and their sibling loyalty
For some other female royalty
She feels bitterly betrayed by her brother
Wonders now what will become of her?

She lowers her head in contemplation
Trying to make sense of the situation
Bo's life is sorted so it seems
Thwarted are her simple dreams

The bare harsh truth leaves her weary
Exhausted sad and somewhat teary
She treks on back to their gloomy room
Her heart swallowed up in a shadow of doom.

CHAPTER VI

Violet is awoken by the medieval clock –
The sound of the crowing cock
Prepares to visit the man at her own risk
In honour of her promise

Out the door she goes tip toes
Into the dark cold street where the wind blows
Hard across her face
She shivers starts to embrace
Her shawl, held tightly in place
As she ventures off at quite a pace
Towards the Copthorn Inn -

Her feet move swiftly down narrow paths
Her body battling the wrath
Of freezing air
Biting and stinging her all the way there

Through strength and sheer determination
She eventually reaches her destination

Hastily she rushes in
The premises of the Inn
Heads confidently to the door
Of the room where she was the night before

Feeling as cold as death
She takes a moment to catch her breath

SHELAAGH

Blows on her hands frozen as ice
Then knocks on the old oak door thrice

Inside the Jeweller is stood poised at night
Gazing through the window at the silvery moonlight
He remains pensive and still

While Violet bobs up and down trying to recover from the chill

She knocks again, listens, hearing naught
Wonders, 'Is it possible he's forgot?'
She bangs hard again, she does not want to leave
If she faces outside she knows she will freeze

'Yes, yes', at last she hears
Like music to her little cold ears

The Jeweller opens the door, stands there tense
An exasperated Violet having lost patience
Ignores the hand stretched politely to greet
La Petite Negress dancing on her feet
Instead his object of desire
Brushes right past him and runs straight to the fire

'Cold! Cold!' She keeps repeating as she rubs her hands together
'Yes, yes, indeed', he replies, 'particularly gruelling weather'

He goes to a pot
Containing stock and a shot
Of whisky that has been on the brew

Gurgling in the jug
Pours some in a mug
'Here', The Frenchman says, 'For you'

Still shaking as she takes the tin cup
And starts to drink to warm herself up
And while she continues to sip and drink
The Jeweller begins to potter and think
How best to create a bright light pool
Around a wooden high top stool

He gathers candles from a wooden box
Uses books and crates as building blocks
To support the way they can
The candle holders in his hand

The candles and holders are put in place
Periodically he glances at the girl face
While trying to assess her height
Then making adjustments to the site

He improvises with white draping
Tailoring and cleverly making
The cloth act as a reflective screen
With mirrors and glassed water to enhance the beam
Of light from the candles lit one by one
Finally he stands back to admire what he has done

When Violet eventually turns around
Her eyes cannot believe the sight she has found
The dull space a magical studio creation

SHELAAGH

She is blown away by the transformation

The man feels proud somewhat light-hearted
Now is anxious to get started

'Are you feeling better?' He asks sympathetically
'Yes sir I am but what are you going to do to me?'

The Jeweller looks her up and down says
'Can you remove your cape?'
Violet responds with a firm retort
'Not 'til you answer me straight!'

'Dear child, no need to fret and bawl
I am going to make a drawing of you that is all'

Violet falters
Her expression alters
'You can draw? Make a picture of me?
For all di world and grandchildren to see?

Amused by her bewilderment
And with a sense of entitlement
The man insists
'Yes, I am an artist'

Violet looks around again
Notices a sketch pad and quill pen
Some inks a fur stole made of sable
And a small easel on the candlelit table

A painted chest sits to the side
Measuring 8 inches tall, 14 inches long and 10 inches wide
Her inquisitive mind inquires in jest
'So tell me sir what's inside the chest?'

The Jeweller turns to her with smiling eyes
Responds dearly, 'Now that's a surprise'

He approaches the fire to stoke
Then gestures for her to remove her cloak

Violet suddenly feeling excited
At the prospect of being documented
Has no trouble slowly removing
This particular article of clothing

He takes the garment from her hand
Places it near the portrait stand
Then quickly on his feet
Returns to guide her to her seat

Carefully negotiating the candle flame
Skilfully leading his dame
To the wooden stool. He helps her onto it
Directs her how to sit
Placing one hand on top the other
Tells her, tilt her head one way then another
Up, down, left, right
Then he adjusts the candlelight

SHELAAGH

He is about to tinker with her dress
But sensing her unrest
Asks, 'What is your name?'
'Dema call me Violet', she doth proclaim

'Ah! Flower –
Vous êtes une petite
Fleur de l'Afrique'
He says as he gently strokes her face, 'African Violet'

Yet
One should note
This was not said as a pun or joke
For the African Violet plant known to we
Had not yet been introduced to this present country
That would not be
For another hundred years in 1893

O sorry, my bad, I digress
From the story of La Petite Negress
At the place
Where the jeweller is invading her space
Tinkering with her frock no less

He opens up the neckline of her cotton dress
To reveal her shoulders and enhance her long slender neck
Violet could protest but evidently thinks what the heck
Why put him in detention
I'm enjoying being the centre of attention

The artist gets her to strike the perfect pose
Then goes
And settles down at his work station
Sparing little time for contemplation
Locks eyes on his muse so raw
Picks up his quill and starts to draw

But no sooner had he put pen to ink
The artist stops again to think

He is bothered by something starts to mumble
Under his breath begins to grumble
Intensely he continues to stare
At the cotton sheath wrapping her hair

'Could you get rid of that thing?'
'Not in a month of Sundays', defiantly she sings
'Violet it's important do not make me wait
Try your best to accommodate'

After a moment's pause she reluctantly she peels
The scarf away and reveals
Her unkempt short woolly dreds
Upon her lice filled nappy head
Now do not be repulsed by this
It is the 18th Century everyone had lice, even the rich!

Violet feeling self-conscious of it
Gives her head a little itch

'Hmm...' the man wonders what to do

SHELAAGH

'How can I improve you?'

He gives her a brush and comb
But seeing her difficulty decides to leave it alone
For the pained expression she was making
While several of the comb's teeth were breaking
When she tried to pull the comb through
Her tight knit curls knotted like glue
Was persuasive enough and clear
That this was not a good idea

So at this point he goes back to the table
Picks up the painted chest and the sable

'Now let's see what's inside the box'
Immediately Violet's wide-eyed gaze locks
On the casket opened using a small key
Its hinged lid lifted carefully

Inside the box glistens. It is full of sparkling jewellery
Made of the most precious metals and gemstones, truly
An amazing sight for the eye to see
A fine collection that one would agree
Was fit for Queens and Kings
Diamond cut necklaces, sapphire gold rings
Ruby brooches, pearl hair pins
Emerald bracelets all types of things

The Jeweller begins to fumble around
Examines various pieces he has found

In the candlelit bright
Subtle glowing night light

He considers carefully what he will choose
To put upon his awaiting muse

Some pieces in mesh and steel
Did not hold much appeal
Others he decides the colour is wrong
Or the chains on some of them too long
Or the designs themselves were far too twee
To bring out the fire in this exotic beauty

Finally he gathers an elite selection
And approaches Violet with his neat collection

He starts to adorn La Petite Negress
Like a richly jewelled Indian Princess
From head to torso he begins
Dressing her hair with jewelled pins
An ornamental comb made of diamonds and pearls
Is placed in the centre of her woolly curls
On her ears lobes looking stunning and bold
A pair of triple dropped diamond earrings in emerald and gold
Then around her neck he attaches lace
On top a rose cut Riviera choker is placed

He holds up a mirror for her to see
The full extent of her natural beauty
She gives herself a toothless smile
Approving of the fashion style

SHELAAGH

Then a heavier set necklace made of diamonds and rubies
Is draped over her chest just beneath these

She stretches her neck like an elegant swan
As he begins to fasten the necklace place on

He continues draping strings of pearls
And chains of gold to decorate the girl's
Torso, then moves to focus on her arms
Covers them with ancient bangles and charms
In an assortment of jade, enamel, gold filigree
Dating as far back as the 13th Century

Then puts an elaborate bracelet round her wrist
Made of gold, diamonds, turquoise and amethyst
And for her delicate petite hand
He prepares several exquisite rings fine and grand

First a Venetian Moretto cameo
Is affixed to one finger adagio
On the fourth an 'Adore' ring set in gold
With an amethyst, diamond, opal, ruby, emerald

In order the first letters of the stones you see
Spell out the word 'adore' colourfully
Then in the centre with resplendent lustre
He slides a large diamond and sapphire cluster

Finally, the top of her dress he lowers to her waist

Drapes the sable around her in a manner of good taste
Holds the fashionable garment securely in place
With a corsage broach made of yellow topaz and paste
Gets her to strike up the perfect pose again
'Hold it there', he says, returns to his pen

'Ah parfait!' he states with a nod and a grin
Now at last he is ready to begin

He looks upon his living sculpture
Enamoured by her magnificent bone structure
Using pen and ink swiftly like a virtuoso
Maps the contours of her head and torso
Paying particular attention to her neck so sweet
Compelling in his eyes most exquisite

Frantically he makes
A series of templates
Deliberately
Absent of jewellery
Later he will fill the centre of the lines
With new and original creative designs

Once done with his rough outlined appraisal
He puts a large mounted canvas upon the easel
Concludes his evening using brush and oils
Capturing the quintessence of the girl's
Magic decked in jewels placed upon and within
Her hair and around her dark brown skin

The gems are made to stand out bright

SHELAAGH

He paints with pleasure and utter delight
Brimming with pride and admiration
For the ornamental goddess his inspiration

'Ah ma Négresse petite Violet
You are so beautiful, so perfect'
He would say. Violet gave no reaction
As she was not feeling the attraction

But by the time he had finished painting the oil
The artist's inner feelings are on the boil

He turns the picture for her to see
Violet overwhelmed gasps, 'Lord! Is that really me?'
She stares with her dark brown eyes opened wide
Like a curious, inquisitive, innocent child

Finding it hard to resist the girl
The artist leans in to kiss her
Several times on the neck and reaches to touch her breast
Violet stops him short, saying firmly, 'Monsieur I need to get dressed'

The artist embarrassed attempts an act of retraction
Apologises profusely for his impulsive action
The jewels on her person he helps disassemble
Then averts his eyes so she can reassemble

The jeweller has been painting into the night
Now it is already morning light

Once fully dressed back in her cape
Violet does not hesitate
To look into the man's eyes all forlorn
In an attempt to exact from him a coin

He gives her three
'You will come back to me'
He says, 'Won't you?'
'Yes sir', she replies, 'I intend to'

And so began this very human
Though unlikely friendship union
Between the upper class dignitary
And this underclass escapee

It soon became a regular thing
For Violet to pose and model bling
She would turn up for weeks at the man's front door
For the artist to produce more and more
Sketches and drawings in the little room there
Sometimes he would concentrate on ornaments for the hair
Other times brooches and bracelets in mind
Or buckles and necklets that he had designed
Or simply on one tiny detailed thing
Like the shape of a stone for an intricate ring

It seemed Violet had found the perfect way
To survive her illegal immigrant stay
But was everything truly alright?
I would have to say not quite...

Chapter VII

As Violet's life was on the trot
The Somerset Case was hotting up
The Somerset Case in all its glory
Was without doubt the biggest news story
So in brief I will now attempt to explain
The background to the victim's pain

A disaffected African slave named James Somerset
Was brought to England by his Virginian master, Charles Stuart
He escaped last year but unfortunately
Was recaptured and imprisoned on the Ann and Mary
That was a ship bound for Jamaica
Somerset had godparents did they give up? Never!
John Marlow, Thomas Walkin and Elizabeth Cade
Were quick off the mark they made
An immediate application to the Kings bench
For a writ of habeas corpus that meant
The ship's captain, Captain Knowles was forced to recall
The victim for the courts to decide once and for all
If it was legal for a master to forcibly
Deport his slave to another country

The Somerset trial was imminent
Buzz around the Case prominent

Somerset had expert legal counsel no less
Among them the most renowned and very best
Lord Charles Kennedy Ruby's master played his part

SHELAAGH

Alongside the likes of Francis Hargrave and Granville Sharp
Methodist activists John and Charles Wesley
Occasionally found time away from their ministry
To join the campaign in support of the victim
As public donations started to flow in

The Kennedy household now a hive of activity
Of friends and associates plotting the strategy
And debating the circumstance in common law
That could change the course of history for evermore

For Bo's girl Ruby the Somerset trial meant
There was less time that could be spent
With her beau Bo
As more meals had to be prepared to go
Upstairs late night at the Kennedy place
To supporters gathered there discussing the Case

Ruby was busy working overtime
Downstairs in the kitchens most of the time
As a result she had little time to fit in
Her usual trips to the Jamaica Inn

Bo's attempts to make a connection
Were all too often met with rejection

Not to be able to see his girl was more than he could bear
Bo became moody started drinking more drove Violet to despair
Seemed Ruby was the only one who could drag him from the mud
Give him a raison d'être, temper his hot fiery blood

Without Ruby's presence in Bo's life his anger he did take
Out on Violet sadly which made her poor heart break

Well, to be honest his outburst would have had more impact
Were it not for the fact
That Violet could escape the misery
With her visits to the man and his jewellery

Nevertheless Bo was determined to find a way to see
His true adorable love Ruby
And resorts to high drama

He wants to tell her of his trauma
He uses his connections in the community
To locate a footman who works for Lord Kennedy
Tells him to tell her of his mental state:

'Mi cain't eat, cain't sleep, cain't think straight
Tell her man in no uncertain terms
That mi heart yearns
To see mi gal
Now!
If she refuses to comply
Tell her I'll climb up high
Upon a ridge
And t'row m'self off London Bridge'

The footman shocked looks upon he, 'Are you delirious?'
Bo's reply, 'No man, tell her so, mi serious!'

SHELAAGH

Well Bo's rhetoric seems to work when Ruby gets word
She takes action talks to her boss of what she has heard
Manages to get a day
Off work to see Bo and play
They arrange a meet
At the market in Old Street

Meanwhile for Violet, everything with the man and she
Was tinkering along swimmingly
Until this event upset the arrangement
Resulting in sudden estrangement

For months the jeweller had been working on a commissioned set
A matching suite of coordinating pieces that was very intricate
On this night he was ready to examine the work in progress
For the first time on the body of his muse La Petite Negress

The fine jewellery arrived in a beautiful silk-lined purple velvet case
That was trimmed with an edging ribbon made of fine lace

The parure featured a number of things
A tiara, necklace, brooch, bracelets and drop earrings
With interchangeable components fashioned with a fine
Figure of eight composition in a classic floral design
Comprising brilliant-cut diamonds set in silver backed with gold
Surrounding pear drop, rich verdant green, emeralds
The stones were high transparency, perfect in hue
Each one of them flawless right the way through
The tiara itself in its design showed versatility
When worn up like an arch or turn down like a V

The necklace had pieces that could be rearranged
So the featured drop pendant could be taken off and changed
Into a brooch likewise the earrings they could be detached
And reassembled carefully and suitably attached
To the necklace in a dress up dress down sort of way
And thus be made appropriate for night and day

By now the man had taken the set
And fashioned them on Violet
Who was comfortably seated, settled and composed
In her elegant modelling pose

It is the 18th Century
So no photography
Instead the artist was happily at play
With his water colours painting away

The pair sat focused unaware
Of the kerfuffle happening downstairs

For that night
A massive fight
Broke out within
The confines of the Copthorn Inn

Now I don't really know what in heavens sparked it
Or how exactly the brawl got started
Something to do with a man I guess
Throwing an insult to another in jest
The second wearing a patch known for his hot headedness

SHELAAGH

Drew out his sword in readiness
The first jumps up like a cocky retard
Withdraws his sword shouts out, 'en garde
Come on, come get me ye one-eyed punk!'
(Didn't help both were incredibly drunk)
The patched man flies at him through the air
Misses by miles being worse for wear
But the excited crowd eggs them on gaily
Much to the anger of the landlady
Who at the top of her voice bellows
'Take your bloody dispute outside you drunken fellows!'
Of course they ignore her and remain indoors
Battling wildly clashing swords
Stumbling over tables knocking down chairs
Creating havoc in the bar downstairs

Then crucially the fight stops being fun
When the first guy attacks the other one
With an almighty swing
Being unstable misses him
Instead knocks an oil lantern off the wall
The oil from the lamp starts to pour
And immediately the light
Ignites

The situation takes an awful turn
As the premises start to burn
The structure made of wood
No way could
Survive or even stand a chance

Against the flames as they start to dance

Patrons all round were scattering running for their lives
Looting in the process stealing cups, plates and knives

Upstairs Violet whose senses are more alert says, 'I think I can smell
smoke'
When the Jeweller says, 'hold still', she replies, 'Sir no! dis ain't no
joke!'

She urges the man, 'Don't hesitate
Go to the door investigate'

He rushes to the door undoes the lock
Opens the door screams out in shock
'Mon Dieu! It looks like hell!
Giant flames attacking the stairwell!'

Violet quickly comes down from her perch to see
Witnessing the inferno senses the urgency
Wastes no time grabbing her things
Rips off the tiara and the earrings
Flings them to the ground
Hears the sound
Of the man's voice, 'Wait! Wait! My jewels', he cries
'My precious jewels!' he screams with tears in his eyes

But Violet sensing the need to go
Quickly makes her exit through window

The Jeweller due to size and weight

SHELAAGH

Is unable to make that escape

He scrambles to recover the jewels from the floor
Puts them in the case made for the parure
Minus the missing pieces
The temperature in the room increases
He holds the case tight
Floorboards now alight
Round and round he turns in panic
Smoke in the room becoming manic

He sees his cape makes a judgement call
A bucket of water sits by the wall
He drops the cape in it to soak
Then wraps himself with the sodden cloak
Bravely attempts to escape the upper floor
Via the hot and dangerous fire filled corridor

Oh what a tragedy, what a sight
The Copthorn Inn up in flames at night
Violet being nifty managed her escape
But what of the man with his soaking cape?
Violet clearly managed to survive
But the Jeweller... is he dead or is he alive?

CHAPTER VIII

Violet having escaped the fire relatively unscathed
Is about to find her brother to tell him she is saved
When she glances down and notices
The emerald bracelets around her wrists
Her hand gravitates towards her neck
Feels the priceless necklace thinks, 'Oh heck!'

Now panicking as to what to do
She knows if her brother knew
He was not a kidder
He would snatch them off her right away and sell them to the highest
    bidder

She wraps her cloak around her in an attempt to conceal the gem
Rushes to find a spot where she can privately remove them

The first bracelet is a little tight
Though she gets it off her wrist alright
With a little struggle she did manage
To remove the second without much damage

The same was not true for the necklace though
Clearly tussling with it so
Being without assistance alone
She is having difficulty on her own
Her frustration mounting as she wants it off fast
So she yanks it off and breaks the clasp
Then proceeds to hides the lot

SHELAAGH

In the hemline of her woven frock

Now for a plan
Go in search of the man
Seems the obvious thing to do
Even though the jewels are worth a bob or two

With the Copthorn Inn burnt to the ground
Alas the man cannot be found

She wonders should she sell the loot
And keep (so to speak) the fruit
Hmm... then the thought flashes by
La Petite's mind's eye

'How strange it would be
For an escapee like me
To be touting around such fine jewellery
An act such as this
Would be too much of a risk
That would surely land me in the pen
Forever Amen!

Besides...'
She decides
'...I've no connections for trading such a jewel
I may be desperate but I'm not a fool
The jewels would cause attention
Not by planned intention
To trade them would not be an easy affair

Like the usual petty crime I do here and there
Furthermore, I'm an illegal alien, imported
And do not wish to be deported
No, leave jewels like these
To professional thieves
I didn't risk mi life and the seas
To end up back in the Colonies'

She reflects for a moment on the brutality
And remembers vividly the cruelty

Considers in retrospect
The circumstance circumspect

Here on the mainland the situation was grim
With poor people hungry looking gaunt and thin
And the smell of the streets difficult to bear
People got frost bite in the cold winter air

But behaviour to her seemed more reasonable
Masters of so-called "Villains" more accountable
With abolitionists vocal about the cause
Everyone under the jurisdiction of mainland laws
(Which, incidentally differed greatly from those
Constitutional Laws created and imposed
In the Colonies with its double standards, hypocrisy
And lawful "exceptions" to the rule of humanity
That permit black people to be brutalized and made
"Slaves" in support of this so-called legal fair trade!)

She remembers her time in Jamaica again

SHELAAGH

Slave masters going crazily insane
The attitude of mainland men
'Out of sight out of mind', back then

And the Governor nearby
Turning a blind eye
To what had become
Torture methods for fun

Like dropping slaves in vats of boiling sugar
Chopping off limbs and stuff even uglier
Randomly picking on blacks seen around
Tying them between trees then chopping them down
Hanging some upside down by the legs
Beating them with chains until they were dead

She was not dreaming up lies
She had witnessed this behaviour with her very eyes
Why do you think she and her brother escaped?
Her brother and she were done with the hate!

Now she and her brother had reached this land
And rooted themselves deeply in the sand
She would rather grow old
Put up with the cold
And the stench of the English street
Than be sent away
To face another day
Of torture in the Colonial heat

Having reviewed all this in her head
Figures the best thing to do instead
Is to hide the jewels somewhere safe
And she happened to know the perfect place
A graveyard site along the boundary
At the rear of the courtyard of the Foundry
She will take them there bury them underground
Hoping that they will never be found

The Jeweller meanwhile though he survived
Is severely burnt - finds himself hospitalized
Fearing he will never see Violet again
Decides to make an insurance claim

In time he files a police report
But never gave much thought
To the implication of his act
The police in turn react
Before long Violet is labelled a thief
Posters are going up in the street
On a public board
That read:

> *"TEN SHILLINGS REWARD*
> *THIEF! Run away from the ſubſcriber*
> *Living in a houſe near Westminster*
> *A Negro girl, ſlight ſet*
> *Reſponds to the name Violet*
> *About five feet two inches high*
> *Black curly hair and jet black eyes*
> *Had on a dark blue cape, woollen ſkirt*

SHELAAGH

Striped petticoat, and chequered ſhirt
Whoever returns her to a gaol anyday
ſhall have the aforesaid reward as pay"

Violet returning from her dig
From whence the jewels are hid
Spots the fixture
A doctored picture
Of the drawing by the man of her face
Hanging up all over the place

Though she does not understand all the words read
She quickly susses out there's a price on her head
She knows she has no option but to flee
For in the local underworld she is a virtual celebrity
Among the crowd who've seen her in the club
With her brother Bo dancing in the pub!
Sooner or later she will be betrayed
By some poor lowlife wanting to get paid
She needs to get out of this town to another
And her only hope now is her younger brother

Quick on her feet
She moves through the street
Concealing her face to avoid recognition
Trying hard not to arouse suspicion
Looking over her shoulder, watching her back
For fear someone may sneak up and attack

Finally at dusk before dark

She locates her brother in the local park
Where he is with Ruby locked in an embrace
She rushes over with urgency and haste
Tugs his arm, yanks him aside, 'Bo'
She says, 'We have to go!
Things have not turned out right
We need to leave this place tonight!'

Bo angered by the interruption
Still manages a polite introduction
Turns to smile at his beauty Ruby
'This is mi sister Violet acting hysterically'

Ruby wanting to be equally polite
Says, 'pleased to meet yah, you're such a delight'

Then Violet's plea is quickly ignored
Bo gets back to business with his broad
Plying Ruby with words of affection
Violet frustrated by the rejection
Tries to pull them apart
But Bo is intent on following his heart

'I'm a "wanted" maid!' She screams, 'you too
Come now Bo! Don't be a fool!'
Bo's retort, 'Sister don't shout
What the hell you talking about'
Violet replies in panic, 'A price is on my head
If we don't leave now we will both be dead'

Bo's heart starts to tremor

SHELAAGH

Caught in a dilemma
Should he reject his sister's cries
Or be firm and remain beside
His true love Ruby
For whom he feels passionately?

Leaving his love behind
Unsure of what he will find
With his sister on the run
As the fugitives they will become
Is a predicament that haunts him
He finds his head and heart fighting

He looks at his sister - panic and fear
To his beauty her smile so sincere
Pauses - counts to ten
His sister pleads with him again...

Finally Bo allows his head to control he
Tells his girl, 'I'm begging, wait for me
I must leave town but I'll return you'll see
When I do I'll marry thee'

He plants one last kiss on Ruby's face
Then grabs Violet by the arm and races out of the place

As both are running down the street
Bo is thinking on his feet
He will need to mobilize a trusty crew
But wonders, 'what the hell did Violet do?'

He soon discovers the beef
When he spots the poster, sees the word "Thief!"

Bo's neither stupid nor is he dim
The man's a jeweller, 'You stole from him
And we need money to get out of town
So where are the jewels you stole from the man?'

He stops to confront her:
'In your hand?' Not there
'Round your wrists?
We need that bounty!' Bo insists

Violet is not prepared to say
They are her security for a rainy day
'Come quickly!' she diverts, 'Bo it's not safe!
Let's get the hell out of this place'

She goes off running down the trail
With her brother Bo hot on her tail
Yelling, 'What you done with the gear?'
Her screaming, 'I'll tell you when we're outta here'

They are running for some time with each other
Then suddenly lose sight of one another
When at a crossroads they reached at night
He ran left and she darted right
Down towards the dock
All of a sudden shock!

SHELAAGH

Violet freezes in an open space
An expression of horror fills her face

In front through the misty haze
A stream of lanterns ablaze
Heartbeat pounding pulse racing
As she catches sight of Black men, woman and children in chains pacing
In pairs along the docks
One man jeering while another mocks
A sight she knows all too well
For she has lived this living hell

Consumed with fear and panic
Brain activity going manic
Her mind knows she has to scram
But her body freezes does not seem like she can
A split second decision is all it will take
To make an undetected clean break
But Violet so taken aback cannot rationalise the scene
All she wants to do is let out scream

She pants heavily and with one deep breath opens her jaw
But all of a sudden feels a giant paw
Wrap around her face
And another grab her waist

Certain she has been captured struggling in fear
A strange deep voice whispers in her ear
'Escapee and wanted Negress if you value your health
Best you do not draw attention to yourself'

With these words the stranger lifts her in the air
And quickly whisks her out of there

Bo is scouring his location
Calling out in desperation
Hoping and praying Violet will appear
He cannot accept she is nowhere near

Reluctant to face up to the fact she has absconded
Hours of searching and she has not responded
He collapses to his knees like a man at the altar
Thus proving blood is truly thicker than water

The breakup of the coalition
Has left Bo in a vulnerable position
Immediately he goes into hiding
Choosing only to confide in
One trusty musician friend
On whom he feels he can depend
To keep him safe and be his earpiece
His concern for Violet does not cease

He still cannot fathom how that night
She completely vanished out of sight
And worries she is alone and in certain danger
Though unaware she is in the hands of a total stranger

The planned escape has gone horribly wrong
With her brother still here and his sister gone
The stranger with Violet is he friend or foe?

SHELAAGH

A tale of happiness or one of woe.

CHAPTER IX

Violet having gone missing in the street
Has been lifted off her feet
By a dark black man wearing light brown breeches
And a long green coat with red coloured stitches
The man is not particularly tall
But the one most notable thing of all
Besides his long dreadlocked hair
Is his strange penetrative stare
From the oddest eyes that looked somewhat askew
One of them brown and the other bright blue

He looks directly into Violet's eyes
Then like a child she is hypnotized
The impact of his charm so deep
Instantly she falls asleep
Like a babe in arms curled up tight
While he carries her carefully into the night
Away from the desolate mart
Places her in his donkey cart
Covers her entire body with hay
Before setting off whistling all the way

Journeying through the night 'til dawn
Into the bright sunny morn
And en route play acting dumb
Whenever he sees someone come
Near, or pass them on their ride
Across the flat green countryside

SHELAAGH

Pied with purple and yellow shields
Of heather blossom and rapeseed fields

A picturesque and scenic view
Of morning dew on variegated hue
He rides through vales, hills, mountain peaks
Brooks, rivers, streams, fresh water creeks
Cutting down dense vegetation
Himself resisting the temptation
To rest while on his tours
Through wooded forests to the Yorkshire Moors

His road trip comes to a sudden stop
When he arrives at a certain spot
Near an aged old oak tree
Where he intends to set his prize free

He lifts the sleepy girl from the cart
Lays her body against the bark
As soon as that is done
Quickly he is gone

When Violet awakes in a fuzzy haze
She does not realize it has been days
She has been out for the count
Then an accented voice on the mount
Startles her

'Psst little girl
Little black maid, little black maid

Over here, don't be afraid'

She turns round to look and sees
A dishevelled Irishman in dirty breeches
Eating an apple that he has just cut
She feels a rumbling in her gut.

The pale faced man is very thin
She begins to recoil from him
'Don't be afraid', he says again
'Don't be afraid I be ye friend'

He offers her a slice of his apple
Then continues to prattle
'Here, bet you're hungry pretty dame
Don't be afraid Tommy's me name...'

She cuts in, 'Where am I?' She asks in a drowsy tone
'Yorkshire,' he says, 'but we best be gone'

Violet suddenly awake
Gives her head a little shake
'Yorkshire? And London Town, how far away?'
Tommy thinks, 'Five days at least I'd have to say
That's on a horse mind ye'

'Five days! On a horse!' she says, 'Now listen to me
I neither can ride nor have a horse, Esquire
So how on God's earth did I land in this Shire?'

Tommy is feeling quite offended

SHELAAGH

By the tone of the girl he has just befriended
'Whoa! Don't get all upset with me'
He says to her vehemently
''Twere Bluey, who brought you here today
Bluey who rescues slaves which runaway
Bluey he's a good man that he be
He's the one who placed you under this tree
He's a friend of all the slaves on the run
Brings them here from whence they've come
And it's my job to take care of them from here'
He looks around checks the coast is clear

'Come!' He gives Violet a little nudge
But Violet refuses to budge
She has no intention entrusting her life
To a man in muddy britches carrying a knife

'Go away!' She cries, 'And let me be'
'I can't'. He says, 'You'll be history
A black faced girl here on the run
You'll stick out like a sore thumb
It's best that you come with me
I swear to God I won't harm thee
Besides I've more apples in me nest
You must be hungry, I guess?'

Violet endures perpetual hunger and bleakness
The want of food her ongoing weakness
She gives in to the man with the cheeky grin
Agrees to go along with him

98

What happens next is hard to conceive
What she sees next is hard to believe

They run to a spot where in the earth
Lies an iron lid disguised as turf
He removes the lid and in the mound
A manhole is dug deep underground
It is about a 3 foot by 3 clandestine cell
Passers-by on the Moors never could tell
And likely never knew of the existence
Of such a safe haven for those needing assistance

'Quick!' he helps her down the pit
Then he himself scrambles into it
The lid is slid back over again
They get settled tightly in the den

The pair begin to share
The stash of apples he has got down there
Her curiosity set aside
Until her hunger is satisfied

She wipes her messy hands on her robe
Then she looks at him and starts to probe

'What's a pale skinned man like you doing living in a ditch
When you could be out there smooching with the rich?'

The man laughs loud, 'Hanging with the rich? Not likely!'
She is taken aback, 'What's so funny? Why so unlikely?'

SHELAAGH

He says, 'You're kidding me! Are you really that thick?
I'm an Irish fellow and a Catholic
And I like you have a price on me head
And every other Protestant wants me dead!
But you...you're a good looking lass that's for sure
What did you do to upset the Law?'

Violet untrusting stays schtum
Looks at Tommy sternly plays dumb

The Irishman responds by giving licence
For an uninterrupted period of silence

Then looks deviously at the pretty miss
And tries to sneak a little kiss
She wriggles free from his embrace
And slaps him hard across his face

Undeterred by her indignation
And being the cause for her consternation
Believing he has done nothing wrong
Pulls her even closer holds her strong

'Why you're a feisty, frigid babe!
How do I melt this icy maid?'
With these words tries once again
To plant a kiss in her curly mane

But melt she surely does not do

Instead she stamps hard on his muddy shoe

'Ouch! – D... D... Damn you! You unplucked goose!
I've many a trick to make you loose
Why do you inflict such violent abuse?'

Still gripping her hard, 'Here's more!' Her cry
As she tries to knee him between the thigh
But fails abysmally so aims her spittle in his eye

'A hen that's fair but base I see, such is your hatred of men!?'
'A hen that demands, let go of me or I swear I'll spit again'

He releases an arm to wipe his face
She tries to break free from his one arm brace
But is restricted by the confines of the narrow space

She stares him down determined to disjoin
Then with her might knees him in the groin
'Argh!' He releases his grip to tend to his tender loin

She is primed to go at him again but he cries, 'No more!
Enough child you win, I greatly admire your valour
But pray tell who in hell are you saving yourself for?'
She responds with contempt, 'Not you, dat is for sure'

He feels he must defend himself, 'Am I such a terrible man
Who has vowed to keep you safe as best I can?'
'No', she says, 'You are just a randy man
With a randy dandy fancy plan!'

SHELAAGH

He chuckles, 'I must say I find you amusing
If not a little bit confusing'
She replies, 'Well I'm glad mi friendly Irish bloke
You find me such a laughable joke...'

Suddenly 'Shush!' he puts his forefinger
To his lips, says to her in a whisper
'We need to stop this banter
I hear horses approaching at a canter'

The men on horses stop to rest
Above their cosy little nest
And feed their animals hay
Before going on their way

Soon daylight above turns into night
Violet tries with mental might
To stay awake inside the mud heap
But soon the two are fast asleep

When Violet opens her eyes
Tommy says he is going out for supplies
'Now you stay here and don't ya move
While I go out to hunt down food
You must stay here with me till dawn
Then Jimmy the horseman will take you on
The next leg of your destiny
To guarantee your safety'

But Violet is defiant and when

102

Tommy has gone and left the den
Thinks, 'I'm not having you
Telling me what to do'

And so she lifts up the lid
On the underground place where she is hid
And just as in a dare
Pops her head out to grab some air

And when she looks around
She notices the beauty over ground
Absorbs the poetry of the landscape
And makes a move to escape
Into its natural scenery
All of a sudden she feels free
Gets carried away with the verse
Starts dancing among the Shepherd's purse

She cannot help it she is seduced by the space
The vast openness of the place
She is dancing joyously
More and more wildly...

But seems she is under a curse
For Violet's timing could not be worse

A Gypsy riding from London Town
Recognizes the girl's checked shirt and blue gown
From the posters spread forth and back
And her dancing days at the Chequered Jack
The bald-headed chap cannot believe his good fortune

SHELAAGH

Grabs a rope waits for an opportune
Moment to catch her like a beast in the zoo
He prepares a kind of lasso
Observes her carefully
Moves towards her stealthily
Then in the middle of her dance
Quickly takes his chance
Whoop-eesh! The slime
Gets her first time

She struggles. Man and lasso win
He quickly hauls her in
She is crying, 'Don't you dare!'
As he carries her to his mare
And secures her to his filly
'Where the hell are you taking me?'

'Ha ha!' He says, 'You are a wanted maid
With a handsome price to be paid
Now, I've got you on my horse
To gaol where you belong of course
Then I'll pick up my 10 shilling reward
And live my life like a happy Lord'

'Let me go!' She yells, 'You horrible rat!'
He continues grinning like a Cheshire cat
'It's a... nothing personal young lady you see
It's just that I have a family
And little mouths to feed
I'm sure you understand my need'

Then off he goes with poor Violet
Riding into the sunset

When Tommy returns and finds Violet disappeared
His heart sinks, eyes fill with tears
He liked the feisty petite maid
Why in heavens could she not behave?
Remain in the dug-out till he came back
Then whatever mishap would not have hap

A couple weeks later back in London Town
Bo still lying low underground
Gets word
From his friend who heard
His sister Violet is being held in a jail
Somewhere North of the Yorkshire Dale...

CHAPTER X

Violet's imprisonment did not happen the way you think
The Gypsy rode to Darlton, Violet on the brink
Begins to cause a scene in the square
Shout, holler and raise her voice there

When she got the opportunity to escape
Instead of running takes the bait
Picks up the nearest thing she can find
Proceeds to clobber the Gypsyman's behind
And through this unsightly rapport
Attracts attention from the Law

Violet is told her actions must cease
Or else be arrested for disturbing the peace
But Violet so enraged refuses
The man sustains even more bruises

It takes three lay members of the constabulary
To get her to lay down her baton calmly
Even then still screaming like a fisherman's wife
She continues to scold make trouble and strife

And eventually is charged with Communis rixatix
Thus to the ducking stool she is affixed

The contraption is designed to humiliate
Women who scold and retaliate
By subjecting the accused female rotter

SHELAAGH

To repeated dunking in a pool of water

Beforehand she is made a fool of in the square
Ceremoniously paraded in the chair
For all to witness her, shamed on the stool
And learn lessons from the spectacle

People were jeering and pointing
Cheering and taunting

Next for the punishment most extreme
Violet is wheeled to the local stream
Dunked over and over in the cold water lake
Until she says she is sorry for her mistake

Seven times no less dunked and held down
Violet feared she was going to drown
And as if that was not enough
There is even more stuff

She is then presented to the magistrate
The Gypsy thinks all this is great
But the magistrate sends him away
Without awarding an ounce of pay

The magistrate asks Violet from whence she came
Violet is unable to explain
'Papers', he insists, 'she must have those'
But poor little Violet knows
She has none she can produce

She looks upon the Judge seemingly obtuse

With no papers to show she is not set loose
Instead he says, 'From what I can deduce
She is an illegal alien and a thief
And as such it is my belief
She should be put in jail
To await the next ship to sail
Back to the Colonies whence, I suspect, she came
And transported forthwith just the same'

'Transportation! No!' Violet screams out in pain
She does not want to go back to the ball and chain
If she had the choice to be deported or hung
She surely would opt to be publicly strung
She would rather be peacefully dead in her grave
Than go back to living her life as a slave

And so the day the magistrate prosecutes
She is thrown in jail with the prostitutes
To wait there until it is her time
To pay the ultimate price, for her crime

When Bo hears this he is visibly distressed
By his sister's interminable mess
And wonders in his heart that day
How he can stop her being shipped away

He believes Ruby's connections are the key
But knows he must plan his strategy
Being a very complicated affair

SHELAAGH

Should he fail it will lead to utter despair

Poor Violet in jail is suffering
Within these walls it is very grim
She is poked and prodded and pawed in there
Girls always wanting to touch her hair
And rub her skin the darkest shade
Wondering whether the colour would fade
Mimicking the way she spoke
Giggling and cracking lewd jokes
Spitting into her drinking cup
Doing what they could to wind her up

But Violet soon earns her stripes
By getting into a ton of fights
Doing what is needed for her survival
Pulling, kicking, biting her rival
Unleashing on them a threatening tirade
Earns the nick-name, "The black plague"
Which to her is OK
Just so long as they stayed away

But one girl's taunts go on forever
Causing Violet's rage to build worse than ever
Until one day she goes utterly berserk
Lashes out at the girl a nasty piece of work
Wrestles her violently to the ground
Then takes her fist starts to pound
And pummel the girl in the head tenfold
Knocks the dear old bitch out cold

110

Immediately she is dragged out from the cell
Amidst the higher decibel
Of screams from the other inmates
The guards come and release the grates
To orchestrate Violet's reassignment
From the crowded cell to solitary confinement

Violet's heart begins to falter
As she faces being done for manslaughter

*

Meanwhile in London causing a sensation
The Somerset Case is dividing the nation
The trial was just about concluding
Charles Stuart and his counsel so arguing:

'James Somerset, a slave is Charles Stuart, the Master's property
Thus has no given right to roam England free
To run away when they crossed the border
And claim otherwise is totally out of order'

Their side believed their case conclusive for sure
Given the statute of "property" law

The Somerset camp on the other hand
Saw a different perspective in legal land

Arguing: 'James Somerset must be released
For he is a man and not a beast!

SHELAAGH

Hence property law should be put aside
The laws for mankind in this case applied'

All await the result in anticipation
Never before had a case threaten recalibration
Of the rights of slaves in the trading nation

Tents pitched in the sand
Each side believing they had the upper hand
Then finally The Lord Chief Justice takes the stand

'All rise'

Everyone shu...shushing then quiet as a mouse
A wave of silence ripples in the house

Tum tid... di... di... tum... tum... tum
The feeling of the heartbeat drum...
For those at the helm the suspense is gruelling
As they await Lord Mansfield's final ruling

The Lord Chief Justice and his staff arise
The Somerset team are in for a surprise
For Lord Mansfield's rule favours the plaintiff that day
Leaving Charles Stuart's legal team in utter dismay

Lord Mansfield so concludes his decision
On the fact Positive Law in England made no provision
That recognized men as property
"And so the Black must be set free"

"Discharged", he said for all to hear
Suddenly an almighty cheer
And loud resounding rapturous applause
Could be heard all round the courtroom doors

The Virginian Master almost choked
The moment he heard these words spoke
Fair and square the battle was fought
And the Master's case was literally thrown out of court!

Did that mean in England all slaves were free?
Hmm...well not exactly...
It meant they had the right to demand wages though
And following the trial some went ahead and did so
Only to find that, the last day they were hired
The following day they found themselves fired!
Out on the street
Struggling to eat
Unpaid
With zero aid
Depressed and distraught
With no support

Many having been forced to leave
Became beggars, vagabonds drunkards and thieves
While others more fortunate with money saved
Bought their freedom in that absurd way

However, despite the said anomaly
The Blacks that day assumed they were free
In no time a group of folk had organized a Ball

SHELAAGH

To celebrate the victory in a public house near Westminster Hall

Bo hears about the dinner and dance
Thinks here's an opportunity and a chance
To come out from under the coop
Blend in with the celebrating group
See Ruby, ask her to assist
In getting clemency for his sis.

Over 200 black men and ladies prepare
To dress up for this elegant affair
To ensure entry to this assembly
Tickets were sold for a handsome fee
The purchase price for the celebratory feast
For both dinner and dance five shillings apiece

Of course Bo did not have that sort of money to pay
Nor did he possess the fancy attire for the day
With ruffles and ruching and that sort of thing
The only way to enter would be for him to sneak in

He would have to go to the river to bathe!
Sharpen his knife to get a close shave
Call on a lady to neatly coif his hair
The way Violet did when she was there

Ruby on the other hand was well equipped it would seem
Because she worked in the household of the winning team
Master Kennedy recognising the importance of the case
In particular to those of her skin colour and race

Agreed to pay for tickets for all the so-called "Negroes"
Living and working in his particular household

Bo figured those dining would need manservants, for sure
Or he could offer his service as a valet at the door
But then how would he get to dance with his date
With she as a guest and he at the gate?
For these events were more formal affairs
With those up top not cavorting with them downstairs

No, he would need to look like a regular guest
If he managed this he could handle the rest
Where would he get a decent coat and hat to take?
Then the thought crosses his mind - "borrow" them from a "mate"

So when the time arose
Bo goes
Quiet as a mouse
Into the drinking house
Where he used to dance
Sneaks upstairs, seizes his chance
To procure some finer garment
From some clueless sergeant

For there was the gent at the Chequered Jack Inn
Drunk as a skunk in a room committing his sin
With one of the regular harlots in the place
Who fortunately for Bo does not register his face

The night of the Ball guests arrive greet each other
In the vestibule as they prepare for supper

SHELAAGH

Men accompanied their ladies
Decked out in their velvet fineries
Collarless coats trimmed with gold braid
In every rainbow colour of every shade
Wearing waistcoats, breeches, silk cravats
Stockings, buckled shoes, some with wigs and hats

Ladies swanned in to the elegant lobby
A sea of pretty fabrics round their body
Swishing and swirling as the women sashayed
In their evening gowns that they themselves had made
From satins and silks whatever they could afford
Some trimmed with lace others embroidered
An array of coloured ballet shoes on every foot
Purses and gloves completed the look

Bo emerges looking exceptionally grand
Wearing stolen clothes from the unsuspecting man
He stands hovering about the door
Trying to figure out a way to enter the hall

He spots a man with three ladies in tow
Catches the eye of one all aglow
Smiles at her she smiles back giggling
He seizes the opportunity to use her to get in

The place is awash with elegant style
As they sauntered down the galleried aisle
Towards the banquet hall to be served

116

The food they paid for and aptly deserved

Bo's charm is working wonders on the innocent girl
Who begs he sit right next to her
However he is not yet well versed in etiquette
As all are seated and prepare to sup

The food is plentiful much to eat
A variety of fish dishes, poultry and meat
Such as partridge, peacock pie, mutton and lamb
Pigeon, beef stew, pea soup and ham
Vegetables laced with butter and thyme
All washed down with some good ale and wine

This was the best meal Bo had seen in his life
He could not be bothered fighting fork and knife
And copy the mannerisms of these pseudo elite
At this blooming rate he never would eat
His style was much more down to earth
Scoff with his fingers given him at birth

This did give rise to some whispering and tutting
Bo just ignored them, continued stuffing
The elders on the table were not impressed
But the innocent girl liked his rough readiness
Simply giggled and laughed at the scene every time
His French beans flew off the table or he spilt his wine

The attention then focused on the leading host
Who led the guest in offering a toast
'To the health of Lord Mansfield and his ruling to be enforced'

SHELAAGH

A chorus of cheers! Then swiftly onto the second course

A lighter meal of fruit tarts and jelly
Washed down this time with some port and sherry

Then finally dessert mainly finger food which meant
Bo was in his element
Picking at dried fruit & nuts, confections and cheese
Pudding with raisons served along with these
More alcohol as well in the form of sweet wine
To conclude the meal that was utterly divine

The guests finish coffee and their petits fours
Then prepare to lead their partners on the dancing floor

Bo's focus is on finding Ruby
But the giggling girl's becoming a liability

He tries to brush her off to circulate on his own
But she is hooked onto him and will not leave him alone
He agrees therefore to one dance of his time
And accompanies her to the dancing line

In the middle of the dance he spots Ruby, makes a break
But for all good intention it is just too late

Ruby has already sighted him dressed undercover
And the girl's arm linked into the arm of her lover
Heartbroken by his perceived philandering
Ruby rushes out wants nothing more to do with him

Bo chases after her
Abandoning the giggling girl

'Ruby!' he calls out, 'Please listen to me
There's nothing going on honestly'

Ruby does not believe him and is intent on chastising
Lashes out and swears at him, convinced he is lying

Bo, once close enough to hold her fondly
And calm her down so he can speak intimately
Says, 'Ruby I love you, you're the best t'ing in mi life
I will love you always and want you to be mi wife
But first I need you to listen, I need you to understand
My Sister Violet been captured and jailed in another part of the land...

When Ruby hears the entire report
She is more sympathetic and less distraught

'I'll talk to Master Kennedy about Violet's case'
Bo accompanies Ruby back to her residence in haste

Ruby having returned to the house prematurely
Provokes Lord Kennedy to ask, 'Why so early?'
He was working in the drawing room on the ground floor
When she came and politely knocked on his door

'Ruby I must say you look pristine and neat
Did no gallant man sweep you off your feet?
Did you not have a good time at the Ball?'

SHELAAGH

'No your Lordship', she replies, 'It's not that at all'

'Then what? I'm curious', he says to her warmly
'Master Kennedy Sir', she says to him formally
'There is an urgent matter to you I wish to confide
Concerning a gentleman friend of mine waiting outside'

Lord Kennedy orders Ruby to invite Bo to join the conversation
Then having heard all the details about Violet's situation
Wastes no time - springs into action. The following day
An application is made to the courts without delay
For a Writ of Habeas Corpus this time for Violet's case
In a matter of days an order is sent to the Northern Gael place.

CHAPTER XI

Violet slumped in the crowded cell
Is not receiving so much hell
Luckily for her the victim came round
After a day or two when things calmed down
Violet was brought back to re-join the masses
Today when the regular guardsman passes
Two unfamiliar guards and an official came
One of them loudly calls out her name:

'Would a female negro by the name of Violet
Identify herself', Violet breaks out in a cold sweat
As she fights her way to the grille
Then stands head down frozen still

'Me sir that's me', she says timidly
'Right then lass you're coming with me'
One guard carefully releases the grate
To ensure the others do not escape
The other squeezes between the pack
To manacle her hands behind her back
Leads her to the stairs slowly she ascends
Dreading the beginning of the end

Her body begins to feel weak and numb
She cannot speak, too overcome
Tears begin to flood her face
As the guards escort her from the jail place
To the waiting stagecoach on the green

SHELAAGH

She is shoved inside and sat between
The official mentioned before
And another fearsome officer of the law

Terrified and visibly shaking at the thought of deportation
And the harsh slave world of segregation
She mentally prepares for humiliation and pain
Possibly having her body branded again
And the rough and tumble of the cold sea
This time in bondage not as an escapee

But days later Violet is not taking a trip
Bolted down on a notorious death ship
As she herself would have thought
But again she is awaiting her day in court
This time in the dreary cells of London's Newgate Prison
But now there is a chance she will be forgiven
And the charges disputed
Eventually commuted

Newgate prison is a damp dark ghastly place
With far too many occupants crammed into the space
The evident lack of sanitation during this time
In itself would seem a despicable crime

A breeding ground for sickness death and diseases
Smells of vomit urine bowels corpses sweat displeases
The overpowering stench on approach to the abode
Has visitors gagging and clenching their nose

Screams, cries, wails of inmates suffering
Are the harrowing sounds that greet you on entering
Mice rats noticeably scrambling around
Fleas lice bedbugs everywhere to be found

Men women children having very little to eat
Crisp cockroaches crunching under their cold bare feet
Corruption rules and bosses seize all the cash they can make
With prison guards perpetually drunk always on the take

Newgate prison has been condemned the authorities feeling the guilt
Are taking action at this time to have the place rebuilt

Bo regularly visits the prison Zoo
To assure Violet Kennedy is doing all he can do
And to bring her food and a little money
To bribe the prison guards if necessary
Cos in Newgate women are particularly vulnerable
Any man can pay to make themselves comfortable
With any woman of their choosing
Fondling sexing and abusing
The victim she having no discourse
And absolutely no recourse

So while there Bo spots an African
Discretely approaches pays the man
Tells him, 'Listen I need mi sister protected
Please brother ensure that she is respected'

The African guard agrees
'Set your mind at ease

SHELAAGH

I will keep watch brother all the while
Your sister is awaiting trial'

As Lord Kennedy works Violet's case like a champ
Bo's starting to win favour in the Kennedy camp
And at one point musters up the courage
To ask the Lord for Ruby's hand in marriage

But his Lordship clearly wants to be very selective
For his employee of whom he is very protective
'What skills do you have? How would you maintain her?
Do you have an income to support the girl?'

Bo reveals, 'Well sir back in Jamaica I was good at farming'
Kennedy finds his response surprisingly disarming

'Hmm... ', he thinks, 'Are you actually
Intending to properly marry?'
'Yes sir', says Bo, 'Dat is my intent'
So the Lord gives him his consent

'Meanwhile', he says, 'starting next week
You can work as a footman to earn your keep
Then after the official registration date
I could offer you both work at my Country Estate'

Bo is ecstatic! His heart is on fire
He is keen to pay down on the ring he desires
So he rushes from there with a skip and a hop
His mind set on revisiting the Jeweller's shop

He arrives the next day at the once familiar door
The ring still displayed in the front of the store
He sees the Jeweller through the window very vaguely
Bo rushes into the shop cavalierly

The Jeweller is sat looking rather hunched
Parchment sheets scattered round him all scrunched
Bo is shocked by the pitiful sight
Of the man bearing scars from that dreadful night
When the fire broke out at the Copthorn Inn
Bo cannot help but feel sorry for him
Even though he seems to be on the mend
Bo cannot and does not pretend
The state of his condition is not bad
A stroke of misfortune was certainly had
The pain of his injuries clearly taking its toll
The Jeweller just is not as perky on the whole

When the Jeweller sees Bo in the shop that day
He reaches for the ring and to Bo to say
'Take the ring, have it for free just tell me
Where your sister happens to be'

He notices a change in Bo's expression
From upbeat down to a kind of depression
'I'm sorry to say my sister is in jail you see
Hoping and praying for clemency

Kind Sir I best be on my way
For her hearing is later on today

SHELAAGH

If she loses her prospects are very grim'
The Jeweller finds the news startling

He thinks for the moment then calls out, 'Wait!
I have the tools to influence her fate'
He gets a fresh parchment sheet and quill
Sits for a moment holds himself still
Then quickly starts to scribble down a note
To the Judge hoping this will sway the vote

> Dear Judge,
> Your honour I write in haste
> In reference to young Violet's case
> And the crimes related to thievery
> I hereby testify that it was me
> Who accused the said accused
> I'm asking now she be excused
> The items Sir had little value no less
> In fact the jewels were worthless
> For this reason I am making a retraction
> I beg of you please take no action
> Signed
> Your humble one
> Gaston

He then carefully folds the appeal
Secures it with a red wax seal
'Quick take me with you', the Jeweller demands
Bo without question obeys his command

Lord Kennedy had Violet's case fast tracked
So she can finally have her life back

Violet is trekked to the Old Bailey across from Newgate
To face another Judge who will determine her fate...

When Gaston arrives he gives the note for the Judge
To Lord Kennedy to hand over to him which he does

Unfortunately, Violet's case does not go smoothly as a bean
In fact the presiding Judge known to be incredibly mean
That day was in a particularly grumpy mood
Having scoffed down so much heavy food
Along with much fine wine the night before
He was barely awake on the court room floor
Burping and belching while court was in session
Due to a severe bout of indigestion
As a result Violet's case was not carefully heard
The judge did not give "the note" the attention it deserved
He hastily decides for all she has done
He will sentence her to be hung!

"Guilty as charged!"

Gavel slaps hard on the sounding block
Violet passes out in total shock
Lord Kennedy and Co. are completely stunned
At the unfathomable disaster unimagined
The Judge wants her quickly removed from there
As he has a number of other cases he needs to hear

SHELAAGH

Lord Kennedy moves to appeal with vengence
Violet is carried back to jail to await her death sentence.

Chapter XII

Violet is still passed out as far one can tell
　　When she is carried to the condemned cell
　　Her limp body lay flat on the ground
As the medic fumbles for snuff to bring her round

Sharply she opens her big eyes
Notices to her surprise
A chink betwixt the cell wall and door
Suddenly like a commodore
She is on her feet ever so quick
Decides to dash and run for it

Across the passageway gunning
Up the concrete stairway running
Back and forth along the corridors of
The different levels of the floors above
Hunting for an opening to make
An effective clean prison break

The prison guards raise the alarm
Now in hot pursuit with firearms

The other inmates even the toughest
Start cheering her on in the heat of the ruckus

Adrenaline carries her to the top
Where she finds a door - but the door is locked
Swifter than the guards on her trail

SHELAAGH

She hears them approaching on her tail

And what is even more shocking
She does not hear the door unlocking
And is even less aware
Of the African gentleman standing there

She is spinning round wondering where to run
Then she sees his hand beckoning her to come

With no time to question she quickly runs to
The man locks back the door once she is through
Then he leads her courageously to a wing
Of a section of the prison they are renovating

He shows her a narrow opening in the wall
That she can squeeze through because she is small
Gives her a leg up, she hoists herself to the light
Forces her body out onto the building site
Once again with momentum and adrenalin
She runs along and clambers down the scaffolding

Meanwhile her loyal team hear of her escape
That now puts her legal case in even worse shape

Gaston responds, 'Has the girl gone mad?'
'My God', says Lord Kennedy, 'This is really bad
I firmly believed
We'd get a reprieve
Now this episode

Rather blows
Her chances of it
I have to admit'

The hunt for Violet continues in the street
With Violet very quick on her feet
Tearing around corners outwitting the posse
By skilfully scaling a weeping willow tree

Now she is observing the scene below
Officials circling with dogs in tow
Scratching their heads wondering, 'what's going on?'
One minute their eyes were on her the next she's gone

The trusty three are amid the crowd on the ground
Hoping she will surface so they can talk her round

But Violet stays hidden from daylight to sunset
When the search is called off by the prison inspectorate
Then when she feels it is safe to come down
She promptly goes into hiding underground

*

Two weeks in hiding Violet is surviving on paltry handouts
Lord Kennedy, Bo and Gaston not knowing her whereabouts
With barely enough food to keep herself going
And signs of malnutrition clearly showing
As the days go on she is not very strong
Consequently her freedom does not last long

Two Saturdays later she is caught begging in the street

SHELAAGH

By a big burly officer standing by her feet

He removes her from her claimed spot in the town
To her cell in the jail only this time she is nailed down
With iron locks and sturdy chains inside
Her chances of reprieve instantly denied
Furthermore it is decided because of her escape
To speed up her execution to an earlier date
Monday morn precisely in two days' time
Cos they never hang on Sunday for any crime

The African gets word to Bo and Lord Kennedy warned
Likewise Gaston the Jeweller is so informed

But with the hanging arranged in such a way
Tomorrow the Sabbath a Holy day
Like a shipwrecked sailor who finds himself marooned
Violet herself is most certainly doomed.

Chapter XIII

Sunday morning service in the Chapel was very grim
Violet in the condemned pews watches the pastor hammering
A message of damnation while the condemned are forced to face
A coffin cruelly placed in the centre of the floor space

A downtrodden Violet is far from concentrating
A kaleidoscope of images fill her mind while ruminating
On her life finally coming to an end at last
She reflects on all the people of her past

Her brother she was bound to from the very start
Once upon a time they were never seen apart
The Impresario who allowed them to dance freely
The Jeweller who chose her to model his Jewellery
Her rescuer Bluey and Tommy who hid her in the dale
The Gypsy who caught her and got her thrown in Jail
The girls who taunted her in the Northern Prison
The African who helped her escape at a time of indecision...

The endlessly long service eventually comes to an end
With the resounding chorus of prisoners shouting, 'AMEN!'

That night in her solitary cell Violet has a dream
In it she saw a light a golden beam
Shining down on a pariah
Sitting alone by a small campfire
The human figure transforms into a beast
Then turns on her to have its feast

SHELAAGH

She finds herself being eaten alive
Then awakes all of a sudden terrified
To the noise of the midnight resounding bell
Rung by the guard crying out words of hell:

"All you that in the condemned hole do lie,
Prepare you for tomorrow you shall die;
Watch all and pray; the hour is drawing near
That you before the Almighty must appear;
Examine well yourselves in time repent,
That you may not to eternal flames be sent.
And when St Sepulchre's Bell in the morning tolls
The Lord above have mercy on your soul"

Violet begins to sweat and shake
Wondering again how to escape
She struggles and strains with all her might
To release herself from the chains that night
She fumbles around for bits and bobs
Hoping to succeed at doing the job
Of picking the locks working till sunrise
But no matter how hard she tries
Despite her efforts and grappling
She simply cannot remove the thing

Monday morn the bolt is released in her cell
She knows the time has come to face her hell
Along "dead man's walk" towards Tyburn gallows
Her chance of life now has truly come to blows

The guards come and enter the space
To remove the irons and escort her from the place
Her footsteps sounding the funeral march
In the dungeon undercroft beneath an arch
She's petrified!
Terrified!
Won't even allow herself to blink
For fear her mind will begin to think
Of the unimaginable horror and abuse
Of the awful n.. n...n...NOooo Not the NOOSE!!!

She screams out the guards ignore her cries
Violet's mind is so preoccupied
Does not realize that day
She is in fact being marched the other way
Not towards Tyburn and the noose
But on her way to be set loose

When they reach the room up top
She is flabbergasted and in total shock
As she just about makes out the kind face
Of Gaston the Jeweller and Bo in the jail place
And she is told from there on she is free
Gaston actually paid an extortionate fee
That morning to the Justice of the Peace
To ensure her unquestionable release

Violet does not know how to respond
She looks on them both simply stunned
Runs over to hug her brother Bo
Sheds tears of happiness not of woe

SHELAAGH

For a moment Bo allows himself to share
His sympathetic side with her there
But does not really want to linger
As he is keen to put his ring on Ruby's finger

He breaks the news slowly to Violet
Who understandably is visibly upset
On hearing his words, 'My life Sis is going in another direction
But dis good man here will bless you with honest affection'

Her benefactor tries to allay her fears
Offers his handkerchief to wipe her tears
But his actions do not soften the blow
And his words do not stem the flow

Violet unsure if what is happening is bad or great
Bo leaves quickly, her benefactor snaps her into shape

'Violet quick we have no time to lose
You need to tell me what you did with the jewels'
'The jewels?' she says vaguely, 'Oui the jewels Violet I need them found'
Violet back to her mischievous self says, 'Di jewels Sah I hid dem
        underground'

Violet takes Gaston to the spot she believes
The jewels are buried beneath the autumn leaves
She uses her hands to burrow through the ground
But somehow the jewels cannot be found

'Um... Perhaps it is not dis place Sah', they try another and another
The same thing again and again Gaston getting ever
So impatient fumbling in the dark
Wonders why Violet didn't think to mark
The exact spot with a brick
Or if not a brick a twig or a stick

''Twas nearly dark and windy Sah but I remember the towers'
The two remain there searching through the night hours

Near daybreak a Geezer and his dog are out for a walk
The handler is struggling with the dog clearly distraught
Frantically burrowing where jewels are hid
The Geezer is wondering what it is?

'What you got there boy?' He says inquisitively
Leans in to inspect more closely
Sees nothing at first scratches his brain
Investigates the hole with the tip of his cane

Taps a couple times then stops
Seems he hit the hidden rocks
He bends down to investigate with his hand
Violet notices him pull something from the land

She sprints over dives at him like a battering ram
Forcing him to fall like a legless lamb

The dog jumps at her in aggressive play
As she tries to save the gems while pushing it away

SHELAAGH

The Geezer gets up fumbles for his cane
And with his stick beats her again and again

Violet so tough does not cower
She has had many a fight with her younger brother
She hits back at him like a savage
In a desperate attempt to retrieve the package

The dog continues snarling and biting
Now the Jeweller comes over to wade in

Violet's benefactor
Now protector
Stealthily acting like a stalker
Creeps up behind the walker
Presses into his back two fingers and a thumb
Says, 'Beat my servant again and I'll shoot you with this gun!'

Immediately the action shunts from ten to zero
With Gaston acting as the classic hero
The walker puts up his hands in surrender
The package tumbles from its defender

Violet quickly grabs the wrapped pack
Rushes to Gaston's side waiting to give it back

'Run quickly!' Gaston says to the Walker, 'Or I'll shoot!'
The Geezer leaves with his dog having missed out on the loot
'I swear to God I'll have your guts for garters!
Shaking his fist he shouts, 'I will press charges!'

You couple of nutters! You crazy pair...'
Violet and Gaston laughing get away from there

'Here', Violet returns the jewellery crudely wrapped in a handkerchief
Immediately moves to defend herself, 'Monsieur I am not a thief'
'I know that child', he says reassuringly
'You've been through a lot', he hugs her warmly

The Jeweller takes her back to his store
Where she has never been before
When she enters there
She begins to gawk and stare
In wonderment at all the silver and gold
Fine jewellery and silverware to be sold

'Monsieur...' she starts. He cuts in rather abrupt
'Violet I am sorry to interrupt
But I need you to listen carefully
These jewels were for an important Royal client you see
Now I need you to help me
Urgently
Reset the stones and repair the things
Unfortunately my hands are suffering
The extent of my injuries so severe
I am finding it too hard to persevere
Alone, I cannot carry on
The sensitivity in my fingers has gone'

Violet takes a moment to surmise
Before she registers her surprise
'Di jewels dat you put upon me

SHELAAGH

Are going to go on Royalty!?'

'Yes', he says, 'I am Gaston Louis Duporte
Famous Jeweller for the Royal Court'
'Oh!
Mi never know'

'And now I need your help for sure
In fact I want a little more
Look here', he hands her a large parcel, 'for you'
Violet looks on suspiciously, 'What d'ya want me to do?'
'Open it', he says, 'look and see what is inside'

Violet begins to unravel the package cannot believe her eyes
A whole new set of fresh clean garments
Monsieur Duporte offers his chair for her to put the items

A beautiful robe with bodice and a skirt made with blue
Floral brocade ribbed fabric with a nice rich hue
The dress is interlaced with tram and organzine
And is worn over a quilted petticoat in cream
Matching socks and hardy footwear there to support her feet
And a linen cloth cap for her head that looks pristine and neat

'Ah Monsieur this is very generous but with respec'
I am not sure dat it is right for me to accep"

'My dear Violet', he continues
'I especially chose you to be my muse
Because you are perfectly petite

With contours most exquisite
But now I would like you to be my wife
I will take care of you for the rest of my life
What do you say? Will you agree?'

She looks at him pauses momentarily...

'I'll have to think about it, I am not sure
I've never been a wife before'

'Ah come! come! How bad could it be
Violet, wedded to a man like me?
I am old and will not live long
You are young and very strong
What I have here will be yours when I'm gone'

'But I know nothing about jewellery'
She says. 'Look' he says, 'I am going to teach thee
If you don't I cannot save thee
They will come and transport you back to your country
Do you understand?' Violet's tone falters, 'I understand I have no
        choice'
Monsieur Duporte's tone alters, 'Choices are for the rich my dear not
        the poor voice'

Violet sadly lowers her head
Thoughtful of the words just said

'Violet, look at me
You do not look happy
I am offering you the opportunity

SHELAAGH

To be legitimately free'

Violet raises her inquisitive eyes
'Will I have papers?' she says to his surprise

'Papers?' He computes, 'Yes indeed
Papers! Yes, more than you need'
She smiles, 'Then be your wife I hereby agree'

'I will have papers! I will have papers!' she bursts out repeatedly
Singing and dancing around the room joyously

Gaston looks lovingly upon his muse
Confused
But is drawn in by her infectious delight
Soon he too is dancing with her that joyful night.

Epilogue

V iolet has changed and seems to appear
Unrecognisable in her new fashioned gear
Monsieur Duporte disposed
Of most of her raggedy clothes
Except her old blue cape
He did try to escape
With that in hand too
But Violet caused a hullabaloo
Insisting it must stay
Not to be thrown away
She had grown very attached to it
From the day she found it in the skip

For the next few weeks Monsieur Duporte and Violet
Work tirelessly to reset
The stones and fix the broken parure
Soon they are able to restore
All the items to their former glory

Once again Violet models the inventory
For the very last time
To check everything sits just fine
Then it is locked away safe
In a new elegant presentation case

Once the set is ready and packed
Monsieur Duporte wastes no time to transact

SHELAAGH

He rides to Buckingham House the next day
To deliver his goods and receive his pay
Leaving Violet, who is now his spouse
At home preparing vegetables and grouse

Violet's marriage to Gaston Louis Duporte
Was not the romantic affair most girls wish for
Instead it had been simple and swift
But she did receive a very nice gift
A jewellery set made of diamonds and pearls
She had more choices of rings than most other girls
But the one that meant most was of the following description
An eighteen carat gold posy ring with the inscription:
"Forever thine thy true love be mine"
This she wore all the time

She adapted well to being a wife
And quite enjoyed married life
Looking after her man
Cooking as much as she can
Tending to his needs
Nursing his injuries
Helping him heal through his medical crisis
Using natural remedies, herbs and spices
Her acquired island knowledge not to be dismissed
She was quite the little herbalist

But not a social butterfly
Not so much through being shy
More because the upper set

144

Were not appreciative of Violet
And she in turn found them most irritating
With their perpetual gossiping and complaining

Occasionally she would be invited to tea
At the homes of elegant ladies dressed in finery
The introductions made her ill at ease
Say one, 'Violet here is from the Colonies'
Say another, 'How very interesting'
She would reply, 'No Mam 'twas disgusting!'

Her head full of contempt and mischief
As she addressed them looking prim and stiff
'Mi was a slave', she'd add and shock them into surprise
 Then relish the embarrassment in their eyes

'How was that?' Someone would say sympathetically
'Delightful!' She would reply sarcastically

And at one particular event got a perverse delight
Giving those gathered a terrible fright
Detailing and acting out all the gruesome bits
Of how she was tortured and how she was whipped
Making the guests seated in their chairs jump
When she began to thump
The table with animated flavour
Reminiscent of "the Masters'" behaviour
Chanting, 'Dat's how it go
Like so! Like so!'

By the end the ladies were fanning themselves fervently

SHELAAGH

The stunned silence loomed till one said, 'More tea?'
Needless to say they did complain
And Violet was not invited there again

She did not care she had no time for the throng
They were always moaning about teeny tiny things wrong
A speck of dust and they felt ill
Violet's life had taken her through the mill
And she had survived
She had not died!

Nevertheless most found her uncouth and sharp shearing
Gaston on the other hand found her cheek endearing

Over time he taught her to read and write
In time she was able to recite
The all-important "neck verse" Psalm 51
To save herself from being hung
(Lest she happened upon the death sentence once he passed on)
In this instance she would speak these words and plead for mercy
Through the mechanism known as "Benefit of Clergy"

She soon became adept at stocktaking
Taking account of the money they were making
Yes, she was quite a little mathematician
Mastering adding, subtraction multiplication and division
And showed a talent for painting and drawing
Which seem to be her natural calling

Violet's fun really came at dark

When she continued to pose for her husband's art
This really brought them closer together
She grew committed to him forever

As time went on he began to heal
To the point where he did not feel
In so much pain and to the extent
He wants to take Violet to an annual event
"The Royal Academy Summer Exhibition"

Violet considers then makes the decision
To go and give her man support
He in turn proudly escorts
His treasured ingénue
To the crowded venue
Exhibiting classic artworks to you and me
But at the time were Contemporary

When many saw Violet they were not polite
But Violet handled herself well, did not fight
With those turning up their noses
Or whispering to another as she supposes
Making snide comments behind her back
Violet commendably deals with the flack
And the awkwardness of the more liberal ones there
Attempting to be somewhat friendly and fair

The room is filled with paintings galore
From the top of the ceiling right down to the floor
As she and her husband are crossing by
One particular portrait catches her eye

SHELAAGH

She stops to examine the largest painting in the hall
The face of the regal figure recognizable to all
Her Glorious, Georgian, Majesty the Queen
But Violet is fixated on something else she has seen

Immediately she thinks back to her poor rotten days
And reflects for a moment on her bad old ways
Amid the wave of gossiping
Violet suddenly gives herself a smug grin

A bigoted woman is to her side
Whispering and making eyes
Violet addresses her like a cheeky scholar
Much to the lady's distaste and horror

'Madam', she says pointing to the Royal portrait above
Of Queen Charlotte that the lady clearly was enamoured of
'The jewels dem you see on She?
Were first of all worn by me!'

The woman looks at her with the eyes of a jackal
As Violet amused begins to cackle
Louder and louder uncontrollably
At the evident irony

'Shush!' Pleads the woman, 'The room is staring at us
Wondering what's so hilarious!'
But Violet does not stop, she continues with cheer
It is the funniest laugh she has had all the year.

ABOUT THE AUTHOR

SHELAAGH is a British writer with a background in musical theatre and film production. She has performed on many musical stages in England including the West End and Royal Opera House and produced the feature film *One Love* starring Kymani Marley and Idris Elba. Her love of poetry began as a child when her mother would recite poetry to her. During those years she entered many verse speaking festivals and became particularly interested in narrative poetry after hearing Robert Browning's *The Pied Piper of Hamlin*. A natural born storyteller *La Petite Negress* marks her writing debut.